FOX, BEWARE!

Fox dropped to a knee. He could see Etienne, stopped on the track, silhouetted hard-edged against the sky. A fresh figure came into view, a dark figure with a dragoon helmet atop a square head. The clink of a saber sounded, then a lantern light flashed. Fox knew the breed. Slowly, cautiously, Fox began to take out his black silk kerchief. Neatly triangled and folded, it held a pistol ball in the center fold.

The lantern light flashed again and Fox saw Etienne's head abruptly haloed. He saw beyond that, to the big horse pistol in the other man's hand. And beyond, Fox saw Etienne's own double-barreled pistol leveled, the barrel gleaming in the light just visible beyond his body. If either man fired it would be a signal shot to the entire garrison!

The Fox Series:

#1 THE PRESS GANG
#2 PRIZE MONEY
#3 SAVAGE SIEGE
#4 TREASURE MAP
#5 SAILOR'S BLOOD
#6 SEA OF GOLD
#7 COURT MARTIAL
#8 BATTLE SMOKE
#9 CUT AND THRUST
#10 BOARDERS AWAY
#11 THE FIRESHIP

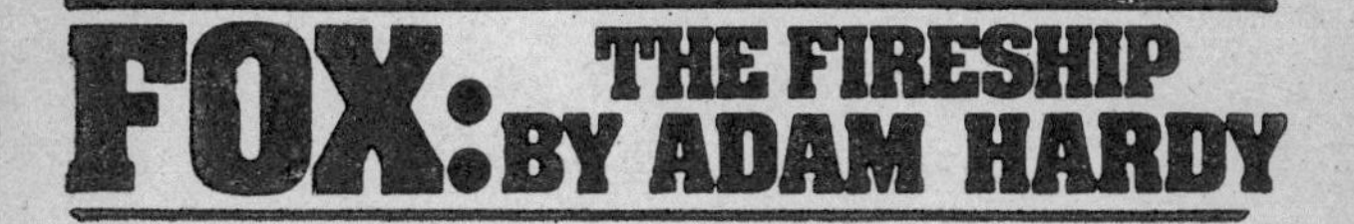

PINNACLE BOOKS • NEW YORK CITY

This is a work of fiction. All the characters and events portrayed in this book are fictional, and any resemblance to real people or incidents is purely coincidental.

FOX: THE FIRESHIP

A Pinnacle Books edition, published by special arrangement with New English Library, Limited, London.

ISBN: 0-523-00845-7

First printing, April 1976

Cover art by Michael Turner

Printed in the United States of America

PINNACLE BOOKS, INC.
275 Madison Avenue
New York, N. Y. 10016

THE FIRESHIP

Chapter One

Fox's mouth filled with water. As he went under he thrust his arms stiffly above his head and kicked savagely with his legs. A primitive beastiality often submerged in Fox broke through now. He wouldn't allow Lionel Grey to drown—or himself, either!

The green swirl of water about him thinned and lightened and his head burst above the surface of the sea and then he could bring his arms down and so cradle the limp body of Grey to him.

Grey looked ghastly. His wound—a searing great gash down his cheek and jaw—still bled. Fox felt the worry over that with the same hopelessness as he felt the loss of his command. The sea water might do Grey's wound good; it had swallowed *Minion* up and taken her and no living eye would ever see her again until the last trump.

"Grab on to the wreckage!" Bellowing and roaring, Fox gave his orders. "Keep closed up!" His crew—those few men left to him by that bastard Lord Lymm—splashed in the sea and clung to bits of *Minion* and so paddled into a group.

Minion had gone.

In her going she had clawed down a damned French lugger and a beautiful French corvette. But it was a court martial for George Abercrombie Fox—always assuming, of course, that he got out of this alive.

Grey was unconscious. Fox looked among the survivors for the hair of that brown just this side of corn gold that would tell him Marianne had come through the battle and the fighting and the sinkings safely. Yes, there she was, hanging on to a spar, her blue eyes wide upon him, her mouth open, her hair streaked down her face like paint.

"George!"

"Hang on, madame. Your countrymen will soon pick us up."

She didn't like the idea of that. Neither did Etienne, her companion and fellow spy, hanging on to the spar at her side.

Fox moved in the sea and took a long look at the second French corvette beating up toward them. This flukey wind kept shifting. The British swirled in the sea where they clung on to spars and barrels and wreckage. The sun shone cheerily and the flukey wind puffed around the compass. It was going to be a fine day, and, over the horizon to the south, that maniac Bonaparte would no doubt be cantering out to review some fresh regiments of poor country bumpkins he'd thrust into gaudy and slip-shod uniforms, and given muskets, and an eagle, and told the ninnys they were soldiers.

Well, George Abercrombie Fox might be thrust along at the point of one of those uniformed bumpkin's bayonets before this day was out, bigod!

The cluster of uninhabited islands called the Remplades was just visible; as the sea lifted and dropped Fox so the rocks came into view and sank again. The four prizes he was supposed to shepherd were hanging about down there, and the one he had noticed previously was already surging toward the men in the water. With the wind boxing the compass it was now more likely than not that the prize, an unhandy but efficient enough coaster, would reach the British before the French corvette.

The corvette's sails slanted in the sunshine. She looked gorgeous. Now, if Fox was commanding her. . . !

Instead, her captain would be sailing back to France with Fox and his crew as prisoners.

They'd probably shoot Etienne and Marianne if left to their own devices. Water slopped at Fox's face, and he gave a heave to Grey to make sure his first lieutenant was not slipping. Well, Fox would have to make sure the Frogs did not find out the truth about Etienne and Marianne . . .

Mr. Watson, the master, looking most bedraggled, shouted and pointed. Fox looked.

The coaster was now quite definitely bearing down on the men in the water. Well, Fox considered; better perhaps to be picked up by a ship with a British crew even if she would immediately be taken back by the French.

Soon the hands were being hefted up the side. Fox saw that Grey was handled with great care, using the rough edge of his tongue to the men heaving him inboard. Fox was not polite.

Here came Etienne and Marianne, splashing on their spar. Fox took a good comfortable grip of Marianne, feeling her roundness and softness and remembering back to the aft cabin of *Minion*, his little gun brig now fathoms under his feet. Bigod! What a thing to have happened!

"George! *Corbleu*–" Marianne insisted on her masquerade as a man despite what the water was doing to her clothes–"George! We are like to be drowned!"

"Up with you, my girl."

Fox shifted his grip and gave her a tremendous shove and the brown arms of the seamen above hoisted and, with a most unmanlike shriek, all aflutter, Marianne went up and over the side. Despite the usual protocol of Naval custom, Fox stayed in the water until he was sure every last one of his crew had been hoisted aboard.

Then he went up like a great ugly tom cat

skipping over the rooftops and, dripping water, landed on the deck of the coaster.

"I am most heartily glad to welcome you aboard, sir."

The naval lieutenant holding out his hand to Fox, a smile disfiguring his face, swam into focus. Fox stared.

He just managed to get his lower jaw tackle to snap shut.

"Lieutenant Blane, sir, temporarily in command of *Alouette*, and although she's a deucedly lubberly old scow, sir, she's a keel and I'm pleased to welcome you aboard."

As though Fox didn't know this tall, ruddy-faced athletic young man was Lieutenant Jack Blane! As though he hadn't seen him hit on the head—twice!—and thrown out of Lord Rowe's coach when it was being perilously held up by a gang of rascally highwaymen. If Jack Blane did not recognize Fox that could only be because at the time of the hold up Fox had been wearing a large and concealing black mask, one of the highwaymen to the life.

Fox realized Blane had repeated himself, and knew he was called upon to say something. Deliberately he turned about, squelching, and looked toward the corvette. That damned flukey wind, no! that blessed flukey wind! had caused the Frenchman to go on to the other tack. He wouldn't be up with them for a space yet. Fox swung back.

"My compliments, Lieutenant Blane. My

thanks for hauling us out of the water. And now—put your command about and get to hell out of here before that bastard of a Frog gulps us all down!"

"Aye aye, sir!" said Blane, jumping, reacting in typical navy way to the crack of harsh authority in Fox's ugly voice.

Blane had a crew of six hands and a master's mate—a tidy number, considering—and the French crew were safely locked way down below. At Blane's bellows, all in good high-handed navy style, the yards came around and the helm went over and *Alouette* started lumbering along like a carthorse.

Fox remembered that the single shot the coasters had fired had come from this vessel. He was wet through, and his coxswain, Tredowan, had had the grace to take off Fox's hideous old hat and hand it to him. Fox grunted. The hat was far too wet for any gentleman to care to wear; George Abercrombie simply slapped it against his thigh a few times and clapped it on his shock of brown hair. The stitches Parson had cobbled in, and that had subsequently been neatly restitched by feminine hands, which brought a fragrant memory or two, had begun to part, so that the old saber cut the hat had taken outside the walls of Acre gaped like the ugly muzzle of a shark.

"Clap on all she'll stand, if you please, Mr. Blane."

"Aye aye, sir. Although we won't get much change from the old lady, I'm afraid."

Thus smoothly was it established just who was now in command.

Taking another critical look back at the beautiful but implacable shape swooping along after them, Fox's subtle and evil brain began working out chances. He did glance at Lieutenant Jack Blane, wondering. Jack Blane's cousin, the remarkably gorgeous red-headed Jenny, who had been having an unpleasant adventure of her own with Lord Rowely in the coach when Fox's cut-throat accomplices had held it up, had recognized Fox at once, despite his use of a black face mask, the moment they'd met again in Tunbridge Wells.

Mind you, a woman had eyes for significant details in a man that another man would never notice. Fox didn't give a damn if Blane did recognize him; just that it would save a lot of tedious explanations if Redeye, as his piratical highwayman's *nom de guerre* had it, remained unrecognized.

Fox saw that his men were getting their breaths back, flopping down on the cluttered deck of the coaster, wet and bedraggled. But they were his men, a fine if rascally crowd, even if they were not yet as fine or as rascally a lot as his old Raccoons. Fox could feel the genuine regret that now he would never have the chance to thrash them into the kind of crew he wanted. These Minions had been badly handled before Fox took command of the gun brig and although they had come a very long way, they were not—and the regret in Fox was all of that fierce and demanding naval tradition of which he was at once contemptuous and savagely proud—they were not yet a crew with whom he could be half-satisfied. Being G. A. Fox he would never, of course, ever be fully satisfied with any crew that could ever sail any ship across the seven oceans.

"She's pulling up on us, sir," said Jack Blane, coming across to Fox. Someone had evidently told Blane just who this tarpaulin officer was, for Fox had been in no frame of mind to bandy civilities, probably Mr. Watson had done the honors. So, now, Blane went on: "You are not that Commander Fox who—" He halted, then, not really looking at Fox, otherwise he most certainly would not have gone on. "I heard about Fox's Patent Boarding Brothel, sir—and—"

Fox did not know whether to keep silent, to explode, to roar and damn, to issue some impossible order—or just simply walk away.

Instead, he said: "Has my first lieutenant been taken care of, Mr. Blane?"

Blane jumped.

"Aye aye, sir. He's been taken below—the lady is with him."

"Good. Call me if the corvette pulls up closer. Keep her as she goes."

Fox turned his back and clattered off down the companionway ladder, fuming.

He wondered through the fury bubbling in him just what that delicious morsel Jenny Blane had been telling her cousin about this tearaway Commander Fox.

Grey was still unconscious. Fox pressed Marianne's shoulder and she looked up, a half smile struggling with her own annoyance at his treatment of her and concern over Grey.

"Thank you, Marianne."

She put her hand up to touch his on her shoulder.

"If that little ship catches us, and we are taken back to France—George—they will shoot us!"

"The Frenchman hasn't caught us yet."

"No—"

"Stop worrying over that sort of nonsense, Marianne. You've come through a hell of a lot already. We'll think of some trick to fool the Bonapartistes, so don't fret."

As he went back on deck he was sardonically aware how easy it was to talk like that, when the facts spoke otherwise. Marianne had called his corvette a "little ship". Well. She was a ship, right enough, and she was small, right enough, compared to a ship of the line. Her twenty twelve-pounders would do this coaster's thin scantlings no good; she was quite big enough for the work in hand.

The Remplades were in fair view now,

their harsh rocks flinging back the waves in a lacing of spray that glinted in that idiotically cheerful sunlight. Fox felt like shaking his fist at the sun, grinning away up there. He felt trapped. He'd fought and now he could do no more. Being G. A. Fox he would go on fighting until past the end, of course; but he was now experiencing all the emotions a fox must feel when those pink-coated idiots set their hounds on it and snapped its neck—if it was lucky. More often than not the poor bloody fox was ripped to shreds.

Fox glared at the corvette.

That's what he wanted to do to her. To serve her as he'd served her consort seemed to him more than he could hope for. Spray blatted inboard and stung his face. He blinked and cursed, quite automatically. His left eye was working well; proof that his inner instincts at least were still battling on. He was perfectly aware all this time of staring back at their pursuer, of making himself stand firmly upon the deck, of making that gargoyle face of his that the eyes of the whole crew were fastened upon impassive. They wanted to know what he intended to do. Already, in his short time, they had come to expect miracles and evilly brilliant stratagems from Commander Fox.

He kept the crew waiting.

If the poor deluded fools didn't recognize now that no miracles or evilly brilliant stratagems were going to save them from a French prison then Fox did not intend to enlighten them yet awhile. Sergeant Dunn had his marines hard at work cleaning their muskets. Well, good for him. That was the best thing to do now, work and not think.

Mind you . . .

George Abercrombie Fox ignored the covert stares of the crew and the even more covert glances of Mr. Blane's men, and took himself off aft. The French had mounted a little pop-gun here, its trucked carriage so positioned that it might be run from larboard quarter to starboard quarter.

The running tackle was ready rigged. The gun that had fired earlier had been the bow chaser. Now Fox stared at the little four-pounder, and over the creaming tumbling wake of *Alouette* at the graceful masts and spars of the corvette, her canvas bellying, driving that elegant hull along after them like a wolf through snow. Yes . . . He'd crippled a corvette with a four-pounder before this. He might again. It was the only thing he could try. Some idea that the previous exertions he had indulged in, the fighting, the boardings, the sinkings and the ducking in the sea, had sapped some of his natural arrogant bloody-mindedness occurred to him.

Bigod! If he, G. A. Fox, couldn't knock a spar off that Froggy over there. . . !

The gunner, Mr. Smith, materialized at

Fox's elbow. Mr. Smith looked impatient, eager, like a terrier held back with the rat in full view.

Recalling his remarks to the gunner about big bangs, Fox, with his ugly face stone cold, said: "I think we might try a little sport, Mr. Smith."

"Aye aye, sir!"

If the gunner had been discommoded by the fighting and his drenching in sea water, he appeared to have overcome that handicap. Fox brightened, and bellowed for men to clap on to the tackles. Despite all, the crew were still anxious to get their whacks in at Johnny Crapaud.

That pleased Fox.

Lieutenant Blane approached, his ruddy face lighting up. "We had a crack, earlier, sir; but these little pop-guns—" He moved his hand through the air, not dismissively but with a phlegmatic resignation.

"Bar shot, Mr. Smith," said Fox. He spoke with a hard deliberateness he forced into his naturally arrogant tones. "These deuced Froggies usually have plenty of the stuff in their shot lockers." He glanced past Mr. Blane, forward, to where the three other coasters were spreading their wings in flight. He spoke now with due concern that what he said would be held against him later, at his court-martial. "I have my duty to protect the prizes, Mr. Blane. I intend to do that." It was all fustian, histrionic stuff;

but it would serve. "We must cripple that corvette if the prizes are to have a chance."

Blane shook his head.

He saw Fox's eyes fix on him, and he drew himself up with a quite unconscious stiffening of his spine.

"Aye aye, sir!"

He could say no more; he needed to say no more.

If his words sounded bombastic, then even that would not be held against him if he succeeded. Fox, always a hard man, knew that any English sea officer would know his duty lay in interposing his own flesh and blood body between the broadsides of his country's enemies and the material objects that country needed to fight and win this eternal damned war. Fox, of course, didn't see things quite in that imbecilic way; but for the sake of his own skin he had to give that impression.

He called to mind that time off the coast of Spain when *Raccoon*, under the command of that cheerful nonentity Sanders, had been engaged on a successful cruise. Fox, with three coasters to deal with, had then crippled a Spanish corvette with a shot from a little brass four-pounder. He recalled that even as he applied the match to the touch hole he had known he was going to be lucky with an unfamiliar gun–had known he was going to hit.

No such welcome presentiments afflicted him now.

He felt a much older, tireder, grayer, man than that Mr. Fox of those days, burning with resentment over losing command of *Raccoon* to Sanders.

The four-pounder was ready. It was an iron piece, probably cast to sail with Noah in the Ark, as inaccurate and unreliable as a witness to a murder. The corvette foamed along in fine style. Fox took the linstock and blew thoughtfully upon the burning match. He bent to peer along the line of metal and saw a white puff break from the bows of the Frenchman.

The roundshot tore into the sea over their larboard bow. So. The range was coming down. He waited, feeling his body going up and down with the motion of the coaster, seeing quite clearly out of both eyes—and that was deuced strange!—and automatically counting the time it was taking those Frog gunners to reload. The next puff of white smoke came in a time that made Fox grant the Frenchmen some aptitude with their weapons. This time the shot fell closer.

Now.

He applied the match on the up-pitch, as the coaster's stern lifted. The gun roared and jetted smoke and crashed back on its trucks. Smith had the men at the work immediately worming, spunging and loading. Fox watched the corvette.

Nothing.

He'd have one more chance and then the coaster would surge alongside and with one broadside settle the issue—finally.

Chapter Two

"You will have to strike, Commander Fox!"

Fox bent to the touch hole again and applied the match with his usual careful precision. The four-pounder cracked off, sharp and spiteful in the morning sunshine.

As an answer, that was more positive and more useful than any bombastic: "I'm damned if I will!"

That shot went nowhere. Fox suspected—no, bigod! he was certain—that this gun was so inaccurate as to be useless until he could sight the fall of shot. He was simply shooting at random, and that made him feel all the more heavily the awful weight of his position. Trapped. Trapped and done for, may the Frogs boil in their own rancid cooking oil.

The bone in the corvette's teeth showed white and glistening. Foam spurted high. She was carrying this damned flukey wind down with her. *Alouette* wallowed along, leaving a broad swathing wash, cream against the greeny-blue.

"You have done all you can, Commander." Etienne spoke again, the anguish in him controlled and yet there, like quicksilver beneath water. "There is nothing left to do but strike!"

The crew was running the four-pounder up again. There would be time for one more crack at the Frog. Then the bowsprit, the forecastle, the waist, of the corvette would overlap. Then . . .

"Why do you not answer, Commander?"

"There is no damned answer I can give. Now step aside, Etienne, whilst I give this useless hunk of iron a last chance."

A mouthful, that, for G. A. Fox in action.

Had there been time he'd have fired short and low so as to spot the shot. He'd assumed that the crack-shot Fox could always master a gun so as to hit—and he could, too—but this piece was hopeless. Now he had one more shot left and then—why, then, he would emulate the fox for which he was named.

He peered along the line of sight. No—wait. Wait. This time he'd let the bastard come in so close he couldn't miss.

He looked back over his shoulder.

"Mr. Blane! I'll trouble you to come about the instant I give the order. Clap all the men you need on to the braces." He must be scowling, for Blane once more showed that conscious stiffening up.

"Aye aye, sir!"

"And make it cheerly now—and damned quick!"

Although time was fleeting by everything seemed to be taking place in slow motion, as though old Father Time nodded over his hour glass. He'd be damnably ready with his great scythe, though, when the time came . . .

The thought of dying came as no novelty to Fox; that specter kept a man company the moment the warps fell away and the canvas slatted home and your ship cast off into deep waters. Death was a familiar ogre to any seaman. But, still, waiting with the smoldering match, with his fierce and ugly face fixed passionately toward the corvette, an obstinate and bloody-minded spirit began once more to invade the scheming and devious mind of George Abercrombie Fox. Scheming and devious he was—aye, and damned cunning, too!—and if he couldn't make this smart corvette captain dance to his tune before he smashed them to kindling, why, then, he'd no right to that black reputation of his.

Thinking this, Fox abruptly realized that his left eye had been closing up with that devilish ring of purple and black, the result of an old and forgotten wound, and now he was seeing with two eyes again. Remarkable, really—all this time which flashed past in mere heartbeats the corvette had been reaching up on them—remarkable, and he'd been about to chuck the sponge in.

He'd wait, now, before he fired, with a

whole world of extra venom, a great discovery that he wasn't anywhere near finished yet. Just before he pressed the light to the touchhole Fox wondered if he really was fit for command. He let concern over others weigh him down when, given his usual self, he didn't give a tinker's damn for anyone at all in the whole wide world, except, of course, for his family of Foxes by the Thames and Captain—and soon to be Major—Rupert Colburn of the Forty-Third. And, too, if he allowed himself the weakness, for Mr. Lionel Grey and Mr. John Carker.

The four-pounder smacked out the gunsmoke blew back and Fox sniffed that battle odor, the perfume of Valhalla, and despite himself his thin licks ricked back into a scowl of such a ferocious zest that he would have soured the milk in the breasts of any wet nurse who clapped eyes on him.

"Now, Mr. Blane!" he bellowed, turning as he yelled and jumping aft along the cluttered deck. "Cheerly now!"

Canvas slatted and banged as the yards went over. Blane was doing a seamanlike job. *Alouette* heeled, swinging into the eye of the wind, the hands hauling and heaving as Fox bellowed at them. She turned, she hung, for a dreadful moment Fox thought they'd missed the turn; then the coaster flew around on to the other tack and so they could straighten out again, running fast.

Fox looked back.

The corvette was swinging, too, surging through the sea, after them as that ferret would be after them, seeking to snap their necks between strong white teeth.

"They didn't fire, sir," said Blane, looking back, his ruddy face one huge smile. "We outfoxed 'em, then, sir. Or, rather, you did, Commander Fox."

"Yes."

Fox flung a look at Blane, and then looked back at the Frenchman. "We'll twist and turn as much as we can, Mr. Blane. We'll keep the bastard from our throats for a time. But it won't last."

Blane had never served with Fox before; but he had heard of him—witness his thinking reference to FPBB—and it was perfectly clear he expected a routine miracle.

The wind gusted, and Fox seized the chance to go about again and then quickly come back to his original course. The Frenchman went on tacking and for a space was standing clear away from *Alouette*. A torrent of jeers and catcalls broke from the hands. Some of them were shaking fists and cutlasses. Fox noted with an approval that fought through his distaste for outbursts like this that the men had hung on to their weapons as the marines had retained their muskets when *Minion* went down, and the corvette that had participated in their destruction.

"Belay that, you heap o' blagskites!"

They subsided; but with clearly evident relish the hands enjoyed the discomfiture of Monsieur Jean Crapeaud.

The game of chase went on for far longer than Fox had any right to expect. He could see the way Marianne held her clenched hands to her breast, anguished each time the corvette almost had them. This was like that foul business some landlubbers had of setting a couple of greyhounds on a rabbit. It might serve those who considered that sport to be in the position of Fox and his people in *Alouette* now. There was only one hound chasing them, true; but she was nimble and her fangs would rip them to matchwood in time.

Time. Fox needed time; but for what?

There was no hope that that elegantly refined bastard Lord Lymm would return now. The gale had not prevented him from continuing with his secret attack. He had taken with him the bulk of Fox's crew, and that was as big a contributory factor to this present evil state as anything. If Lymm, who commanded the small squadron of gun vessels of which *Minion* had been a discarded member, had decided to give up the attack, he would have returned by now.

The sea remained empty of all but the eager questing shape of the corvette, her canvas filled and shining as she twisted and turned after the lurching *Alouette*, and the old coaster herself, running and dodging.

Fox's art of seamanship was put to the most severe test. Twice the corvette let loose and on each occasion chunks of the coaster were blown away. No one was hurt. But this could not go on. Everyone knew—and most of all that captain over there, a Frenchman no doubt swearing away as he drove his ship after this infuriating little cockleshell.

Marianne was trying to catch Fox's eye. He resolutely refused to acknowledge her presence. She had proved herself to be a brave woman already; Fox found something displeasing to him in the way she exclaimed in delight at each twist and turn of *Alouette*, escaping, as she phrased it, from the fangs of the Corsican Tyrant. With a dose of all his old cynicism, Fox, even as he maneuvered the coaster to keep her away from those damned iron guns of the Frenchman, realized that she was expecting the miracle, also. If this situation was being written up by some wordsmith for a popular ballad the intrepid British would outsmart the French and lure them on to the rocks, or hurl a keg of gunpowder at them, or do something that was really all moonshine to escape. Real life, real naval life which had without doubt been the most important single factor in nurturing the youth and man who was now G. A. Fox, turned on a question of duty and courage and blind fanatical heroism, at times; but, most of all to a sea officer like Fox, it turned on the nice calculation of chances, of odds, of long and hard-won experience. This coaster could never outrun the corvette. The French captain had already proved by his seamanship he would not be drawn like a loon on to the rocks. Anyway, the coaster probably drew as much or more than the corvette. As for a keg of gunpowder—Fox had done that, bigod; but it was not on in these circumstances. The Frenchman was going to have them in this situation.

Finally.

Able Seaman Landsdowne, that sailor with the shock of fair hair and the cheeky smile he dare never let slip on to his face when an officer was present, that same Landsdowne who was turning into almost as fine a lookout as Wilson, the old Raccoon who was reputed to have the finest pair of eyes in the fleet, that Landsdowne now perched in the crosstrees let out a bellow that made Marianne jump.

"Deck there! Sail ho! Fine on the looward bow!"

Mr. Midshipman Gruber, for all the experience he was cramming into the lively brain behind that freckled face, could not stop himself from jumping up the ratlines of the larboard shrouds. Before he was up three of the ratlines he was already conscious of what he was doing, as Fox saw with a harsh glimmer of malice, and so the lad jumped down again, confounded.

"What d'ye make of her?" shouted up Blane.

That was quite unnecessary. Landsdowne would shout down to the deck all the information as it appeared.

"Cain't tell yet, sir. She's royals set."

That sounded ominous.

Many and many a British captain would never set his royals from dockyard to dockyard, too frightened that something might carry away, or too stingy to stand the cost.

Everyone waited. The corvette tried another pass and Fox put *Alouette* through a crazy series of evolutions and took a spattering of roundshot through the mainsail. Lines parted.

"Get on to those halyards!" roared Fox. If he was to be sunk or taken, he'd do it with a ship under him and not a mishmash or rubbish. Mr. MacMillan, the boatswain, belted into the work. *Alouette* floundered on. The corvette tacked and Fox watched her with his evil eyes, calculating. He'd already sized up the sailing points of the Frenchman, and was taking full advantage of the weakest aspects of the corvette's performance.

Landsdowne hailed again.

"A ship, sir–corvette–"

Blane let out a profane string of oaths.

Mr. Watson tut-tutted, looking flustered.

Fox turned to Gruber.

"Take yourself and a glass aloft, Mr. Gruber."

"Aye aye, sir!"

There was going to be precious little room for both of them in the coaster's crosstrees.

Marianne's hands were wringing together, pressed against her breasts. Fox wanted to step over to her and gently draw her fists away and calm her. He remained where he was, his beaked nose jutting, his rat-trap mouth firmed shut, his whole chunky body purposive and giving the impression of trembling controlled energy, reined in under an iron discipline.

He looked at the Frenchman.

A hazy crimping of purple began around his left eye, narrowing his vision, making him want to fling his hat on the deck and jump on it. Treatment like that could only improve his headgear.

He watched the Frenchman.

Gruber yelled.

But Fox already knew.

The French corvette heeled away, her canvas drawing, her masts leaning, her flags stiff. She made a fantastically beautiful picture, the spume flying, the sun glinting from her sails, the whole rapturous mystery of a tall sailing ship plunging boldly through the sea.

All that beauty was made tenfold more superb for Fox by the movements of the corvette. She was turning tail. She was running!

Gruber yelled: "She's British! A British corvette!"

"Goddamme!" said Blane, startled. "That'll be Commander Purvis, for a fiver!"

Fox never bet on a dead loser.

Blane turned to him, smiling, burbling with good humor. "Commander Purvis, sir. I have the honor to be his third. I was put in command of these coasters by Lord Lymm—"

"Quite," said Fox. He had not failed to notice the way Blane's nostrils crimped when he mentioned Captain Lord Lymm. Truth to tell, apart from his cronies, was Lord Lymm even tolerated by anyone in the Navy?

Soon what had appeared to Able Seaman Landsdowne as merely a tiny white triangle, a mere glinting speck against the horizon, appeared to Fox as he stood, chunky, four square, and now with his hands clumped up into the small of his back. He felt he ought to stand like that at this time.

The corvette's royals, top-gallants and topsails swam up into view, then her courses, and finally that lean black hull burst over the horizon and, seemingly in moments, she was surging up to them, a more beautiful sight even than the departed Frenchman.

"*Pike*," said Lieutenant Blane. He looked at his ship with great complacency.

Fox understood that.

Pike was, indeed, a beauty, with her

thirty thirty-two-pounder carronades and speed and nimbleness enough to get in close enough for their smashing power to be effective. Fox would not sigh; but he lusted after her on her like.

Now there would be no prison in France, no firing squad for Marianne and Etienne. They would once again be able to take up their careers in the shadowy and mysterious business of spying against Bonaparte. As for Fox—well, he would go back to face a court-martial. Commander Purvis of *Pike* brought fresh orders for Fox; he was to escort the prizes back. The attack had not been successful—at this Fox's thin lips ricked into an unholy grimace—and with a reduced crew *Minion* could best serve on that duty. *Minion*, Fox said with a hard bitterness, lay at the bottom of the English Channel. Still, he was alive and going home.

It seemed that Fox's miracle had occurred, after all.

Chapter Three

A very great deal of business remained to be concluded once the tiresome ordeal of the court-martial had been pushed out of the way. Whatever he might have expected, Fox had never, in his wildest dreams, expected what happened to befall him.

Despite his own crusty, rough-bark nature, it seemed he did have friends.

Whilst he knew that that was not so—how could it be, given the circumstances?—he was fully prepared to make hay whilst the sun shone and to take every advantage he could. To do anything less would be to break faith with his responsibilities, which with the addition of further babies to the family down by the Thames, grew rather than lessened.

Any captain losing his command must expect court-martial proceedings to pronounce upon his conduct. The whole truth might never come out; corruption might conceal; venomous hatred might pervert the course of justice; but, in general, those officers sitting as the court were experienced men able to see past the mist of words to the realities of the actions. Fox had no fears from this court-martial if the facts were presented straight; he had very great apprehension that in the distortion of facts and in the suppression of some of the evidence, he might be done irreparable harm.

Commander Purvis of *Pike* had presented his warrant appointing him Provost Marshal on the occasion in due form. Purvis was short and square. He was no taller than Fox although with a much more pronounced tumble-home, and his side-whiskers bristled with that bulldog British courage that made Fox at once respectful of the man's tenacity and courage, and despairing of his block-headedness. Purvis did everything with a meticulous attention, and all the time he appeared to be acting a kind of charade, in a haze of detail and order and protocol. He was far more at home, it was clear, on the quarterdeck than in the closeted confines of a court-martial.

The court-martial wheeled its ordained way. Fox had drawn up his list of witnesses. Those members of his crew of *Minion* who were to hand. Lieutenant Jack Blane. He could not call Captain Lord Lymm.

To his consternation—and that was not too strong a word to apply to G. A. Fox at that moment of disaster—he found Lord Lymm sitting as a captain among the five sitting in judgement upon him.

He'd weathered a court-martial before this where one of the court had been an implacable enemy. Captain Lemuel Stone—Toady Stone—had done his best to convict Fox and only the timely arrival of his crew had saved him.

This time he had to face Lord Lymm.

He wondered as the proceedings wended on their dreary way if, assuming he won free, Lymm would have him beaten up by his barge's crew as Stone had done.

There was a score to settle there—it was all down in the little black book—that would one day be paid.

He did not know three of the other captains—Tompkins of *Surefire*, Patricks of *Jezebel*, and Hodges of the dockyard—but the fifth, Captain Andrew Kinglake, was known to him from the old days in *Invulnerable*. Kinglake had been a midshipman then. Well, that was how promotion went in the Service; Fox did not know what Kinglake's interest was; he did know the man must possess interest.

Kinglake looked hardly different at all. He had filled out, his fair hair was as wild and romantic as ever, with kiss curls cut back with an artful appearance of exactitude, as though the gallant sea officer sought to cut out any suggestion of romanticism in his nature, for that very romanticism to resist and show through with its own spirit. He was commanding a smart thirty-two-gun frigate now, and was very much on top of the world. He hardly glanced at Fox, standing in his shabby best, and kept his eyes fixed on the papers before him at the long table.

The proceedings proceeded.

Evidence was given and taken. Fox's reports were referred to. He tended to become impatient at bumblings; but he must retain as cool a head now as ever he managed to do under fire. The words he had spoken against this very day were repeated. The Deputy Judge Advocate did his duty with a dry rustling, a pair of flies buzzed annoyingly in the slanting rays of sun, the sword gleamed.

Fox had accepted the offer of the loan of a sword from Lieutenant Johnson, second of *Pike*. This was a modern sword, the naval sword based on the Light Cavalry weapon established by a Royal Warrant of the fourteenth of November 1796 giving regulations governing the design and pattern of swords of the cavalry. Fox's mind dwelt on swords and weapons as the Deputy Judge Advocate droned and rustled, the flies buzzed, and evidence was given. The sword was curved—well, Fox knew that a curved sword was fine for cutting purposes—it was 32½ or 33 inches in a straight line from the point to the hilt and the curve at the center was 1¾ inches from the straight line. The breadth of 1½ inches at the shoulder and the thickness of ⅜ inch gave a substantial weapon. Fox had not been able to get his own five-ball sword, nowadays an old-fashioned sword, out of pawn in time for the court-martial. Anyway, he doubted if he could raise the wind to do that. By an irony of that black fate that dogged him, his possession in pawn might be retrieved; he'd never get back his stuff from poor sunk *Minion*.

With his own possessions had gone down the logs of his command.

The court took him through his report, and Lymm, still smarting under his rebuff at Point Avenglas, wanted to push on to the action leading to the loss of *Minion*. Lymm had taken his squadron in to Point Avenglas, that gale had broomed up channel, and by the time he had collected his command about him—collected his wits, was how Jack Blane expressed it, telling Fox—the opportunity had gone. The subsequent attack had been repulsed.

Lymm had taken most of Fox's crew to augment the other gun vessels in the attack. Fox felt he ought to make the most of that, for had he had even a few more men he would have taken the Frenchmen that much quicker, been in a better position to resist the last and fatal attack.

"So you were badly beaten by a lugger, Commander Fox?" Lymm's face looked blank with that shiny blackness, that fixed rigidity, that denotes the most enormous inward grimace of satisfaction being smothered by caution and contempt.

"My report—" began Fox.

"Answer the question!" said Lymm. He spoke with the curtness his kind habitually used with underlings.

Tompkins of *Surefire*, acting as President, appeared to Fox very much a broken reed. As was so often with big men on ship's rations he had run to fat, and he kept mopping his brow in the growing heat of the day. The weather would remain hot for a spell; it always seemed to turn colder after Fox's birthday and most of the men present were sweating in their stiff uniforms. Starting at eight o'clock with the gun and the flag, the court-martial would be got over as fast as possible for each case—for Fox was not the only culprit up today to face his doom.

"It was not the lugger that did the damage, my lord—"

Lymm went ranting on, and Fox saw that the black bastard was adroitly bringing the subject of just who had caused the loss of *Minion* to hinge on the technicality of whether it was the lugger or the corvette that had caused the damage.

Fox knew the answer to that, well enough.

"After the Frenchman shot away my foremast and bowsprit we came together—"

Tompkins, rather hazily, said: "The feller had the range of you, then, of course?"

Quite patiently, Fox said: "Yes, sir. He

had long twenty-fours and long nines. We had carronades."

"I see. Please go on."

"There's no need to go into that any further," said Lymm. He was acting as a lord of the realm and not as a naval captain, that was apparent to everyone. Tompkins flushed up; but he did not choose to reply directly. Lymm went on speaking in his arrogant voice: "You were signally beaten by a miserable lugger, and the corvette finished you off."

Fox guessed that Lymm was thinking back to that time in *Duchess* when a lugger had made them look fools, and Lymm—Lieutenant Charles Beckworth as then was—had hidden below pleading a wound that was nothing at all.

"We took the lugger, my lord," said Fox. "We were shorthanded—"

Lymm roared out angrily, and struck his clenched fist against the table.

"Goddamme, man! I don't want to hear anymore of your whining excuses. You are a disgrace to the Navy! Any commander worthy of the name would have smashed up the lugger. You had thirty-two-pounder carronades, had you not?"

"Yes, my lord—but—"

Lymm waved him down with his left hand which held a lace kerchief. It was a most elegant gesture; it was also a most insulting gesture. Fox did not flush. But his eyes must have revealed more than he cared, for Captain Patricks, of *Jezebel*, put a thin hand to his chin, and said: "You are the same Commander Fox who was—concerned—with what I believe is now referred to as Fox's Patent Boarding Brothel?"

Fox could only reply, "Yes, sir."

"I see. Then I have heard of you, Commander Fox."

Well, and here Fox kept his face straight, whatever the gallant captain had heard could only be bad. Even though FPBB had been instrumental in capturing a Spanish first-rate three decker, the ship had burned, the old *Maria* had burned, and there was nothing to show for that exploit. Like most of Fox's devilish exploits, there was little to show for them at the end.

Captain Patricks, who did not look a well man, for his thin face showed a betraying yellow tinge, nodded at this, and made a notation before him.

"All this means nothing," betrayed Lymm. He was acting not as a mere member of the court, that was clear. Tompkins was quite incapable of reining in the temper of the noble lord, that was equally clear. Fox began to see he was going to get a rough ride here. Lymm would see he was condemned and broken and turned off, sent to rot on the beach forever. "The man has confessed he was beat by a mere *chasse-marée*, and that means he did not exert himself to the utmost. That is what we are here to prove, is it not, gentlemen?"

Hodges, of the dockyard, a heavy-jowled man with pouched eyes and a uniform buttoned up in the new fashion so that he looked a straw-filled dummy, nodded ponderously.

"Indeed, my lord, it begins to look that way, to be sure."

Tompkins said something to Hodges in a low voice, for Hodges nodded and let his gross body slump back in his chair.

So that put Hodges right at the bottom of the pecking order, without regard to seniority, for Lymm was fully capable of smashing a man no matter the difference in their years on the list. Unless that man had as powerful a set of friends as Lymm so clearly boasted . . .

The scene had been set, the actors had appeared and played their parts. As far as Fox could see the play was nearly over. His witnesses were scarcely going to discredit the massive case Lymm was building in his bludgeoning way.

Lymm went on hammering at the point that Fox had failed to beat a mere lugger. Given in these bald words, Fox could see how he himself would react. No British sea officer was going to allow himself to be beaten by a French *chasse-marée* when in command of a vessel of superior force. That the facts were very different meant nothing beside the hammering force of Lymm's arguments. Tompkins at least, as Fox could see with dreadful clarity, was convinced.

The crux of the matter came when Lymm, contemptuous now, declared that Fox had not exerted every effort in the fight, and, that being the case, no further questions were necessary.

Captain Kinglake looked up. He had scarcely spoken. He gave Fox a single searching glance.

"I have a question I would like to put to the prisoner."

"Very well, Kinglake," said Lymm, very much the noble lord. "But for God's sake do not waste more of the court's time. We have three more of these confoundedly boring businesses to get through before midday."

Without a direct answer to Lymm, Kinglake turned to Fox.

"Now, Commander Fox, as I understand it, your command–*Minion*–was a gun vessel, armed with thirty-two-pounder carronades?"

"Yes, sir."

"And the *chasse-marée*, you say–"

"Come, come, Captain Kinglake!" brayed Lymm. "We all know what *Minion* was. Is this relevant?"

Kinglake, thus directly challenged, must make reply. His fair rebellious hair gleamed in the slanting sun beams. His face remained composed, white and deadly. Fox saw the little pinching in at the sides of his nostrils.

"Yes, sir," said Kinglake in a cold voice that made Fox, for one, sit up. "I wish to establish the relative strengths of *Minion* and the first Frenchman Commander Fox fought." At his use of the simple "sir" Lymm—who insisted always on being addressed as "my lord"—drew his eyebrows down and his fingers beat on the table. Before he could let rip with the expected outburst, Kinglake went on. "We all know these damned French luggers. Fast, handy beasts. Long twenty-four-pounders, eh, Commander Fox?"

"Yes, sir."

Patricks, of *Jezebel*, moved a yellow hand through the air before his face. "Aye, we know those damned French *chasse-marées*. Run rings around you and knock your spars away. And they pack 'em with men, Goddamn 'em all!"

"I should like the court to take notice that Commander Fox's vessel was a gun vessel, and we all know the weatherly qualities of those." Kinglake no longer looked at Fox. He looked at a point in space beyond the center of his waistcoat and he spoke in that icy voice. "Commander Fox by a stratagem managed to unrig the lugger. A shot brought his foremast and bowsprit down and the two vessels came together. There was then no opportunity for you to stand off and hammer him with your carronades, Commander Fox?"

"No, sir."

Hodges, no doubt feeling out of it, and desirous of getting on to the record his fitness for a sea-going command instead of the dockyard, said: "Then why did you not board at once, Commander Fox? We all know Johnny don't stand against a British crew, eh? Eh?"

"We did board, sir. We took the lugger—"

Lymm did not like the turn of events.

"We know all that. It is in your report." The gesture of the lace handkerchief effectively dismissed Fox's report as rubbish. "You were so long about it the corvette had ample time to beat you."

Fox opened his mouth. Kinglake shot him a long hard look, and Fox closed his mouth.

Kinglake sat up in his chair. "You were a long time in overcoming resistance in the lugger, Commander Fox, your report indicates you were forced to turn a French nine-pounder on the crew. Surely you could have taken the vessel with a rush?"

"Yes," put in Patricks. "A good spirited rush forrard would have put the lugger in your hands immediately. It's what any sea officer would have done."

Fox looked at them. These men knew what sea fighting was all about—all, that is, except Lymm, who although he had been in engagement had not, to Fox's knowledge, ever actively taken part. They would be genuinely incensed that a British naval officer had not carried the lugger. Kinglake was looking at him now, those fair curls a blaze in a shaft of sunlight. Kinglake nodded. The sunlight reflecting from his hair shifted and danced and swam. He nodded–and Fox understood.

"We would have carried the lugger," he said, in a voice somewhat louder than was strictly necessary in the great aft cabin. He was aware of a stiffening up among those present. The quill squealed across paper, the flies buzzed, the slop of water overside sounded suddenly louder. "But I had very few men left to me. My crew had been stripped. We were so seriously undermanned I could either sail or fight; not both. My crew–the majority–had been taken out of *Minion* for an expedition by the senior officer."

Patricks jerked forward. Hodges coughed and wiped his forehead. Tompkins looked down at his hands, and opened his mouth. Lymm's mouth was already open to bellow something, anything, to ride over the awkward situation.

Before either could speak, Kinglake said: "You had only a handful of men, Commander Fox? I see. Your crew had been stripped from you, by your senior officer. Tell the court who that senior officer was, please, Commander Fox."

Chapter Four

That proved the turning point.

There was much to follow, and Fox heard Lieutenant Jack Blane declaring that he had never witnessed a more gallant or a more skilful or a more courageous fight than the one put up by Commander Fox and his handful of men against vastly superior odds. Oh, yes, through a pinkish haze that enveloped his eyesight and that had nothing whatsoever to do with old and forgotten wounds, Fox saw the rest of the proceedings through. So he *did* have friends. He had never believed it. But he must have, for Captain Kinglake made point after point in his favor. Captain Patricks concurred with an exhausted air that, all the same, indicated where his sympathies lay. That was two out of the five. Hodges was the least of those three; Fox fancied that Tompkins might venture to reassert himself when it came to the verdict.

Just how it went as the five captains discussed the case Fox would probably never know.

He waited and despite all his coolness, his iron indifference to the nincompoops and the titled tomfools in the Service, idiots who denied common justice and chances of promotion to honest and skilful sea officers, he felt the fretful feverishness of the condemned.

Commander Purvis, of *Pike*, could not sit still as they waited to be summoned back.

"By God, sir!" exclaimed Purvis, his short stout body energetically pacing the cramped space. "They can't find you guilty; 'Pon my word, it ain't possible, Commander Fox."

"I sincerely hope you are correct. But, I believe you are aware of certain–irregularities–?"

"May God strike his innards from him!" burst out Purvis. "If the Navy is to be run by the likes o' him, then I'll look at the beach with a very different eye, sir, a very different eye!"

Strange, considered Fox, how in disliking one man, two might be drawn together.

There was no doubt of the contempt and the scorn in which Captain Lord Lymm was held by the captain and crew of *Pike*. There had been no grand entrance of Commander Fox into the great cabin for the court-martial followed by his officers, for Grey was in the infirmary, mending nicely, but with the most savagely persistent headache. Fox had been up to him every day, and had sat, and mumbled a little, and Grey had tried to be cheerful. Fox felt now all the concern for Grey he supposed he would normally expend on himself. He had seen the dreadful effects resulting from a blow on the head or face; God knew if Grey would recover or not. Of one thing Fox was aware; Grey would henceforth have a scar down his face. Mind you, for such a handsome devil as Lionel Grey, that scar would merely turn what had been a remarkably handsome face into a face at once powerful as well as handsome. The women could go mad over a man with a facial scar like that, a scar breathing of romance and adventure, and not in the slightest way disfiguring.

Fox wouldn't want it any other way for Grey. Had Grey been able to give his evidence—and he had tried, of course, and his disposition had subsequently been read into the record to support and substantiate the glowing account given by Blane—Fox wondered how Grey would have handled Lymm. He'd never stand in fear of the bastard, as so many did.

But this Captain Kinglake, now . . .

Fox had pondered this long and long. He wondered if the subtle hand of Admiral Cloughton lay at the back of it. After all, Kinglake had been a midshipman in *Invulnerable* when Cloughton commanded her. H'mm. This mysterious friend Fox now felt convinced was exercising his efforts on his behalf might be Admiral Cloughton, after all.

After all . . . That was poor gratitude. Fox knew that Cloughton regarded him with deep suspicion; but the old maniac with his coughing and choking and his drinking knew, also, that Fox had saved his bacon–twice. For, surmised G. A. Fox in his sour way, by this time Cloughton must have put two and two together and come up with the four that equalled the saving of *Invulnerable* with the mischievous activities of Lieutenant Fox.

Knowing Cloughton, Fox had a shrewd idea the old devil would have spoken to the warrant officers of *Minion*. During the court-martial the warrant officers had given their evidence, which had of necessity been of a technical nature to support the deposition of Lieutenant Grey. Evidence of position, the state of *Minion*, what masts and spars had been shot away, exact times for each occurrence, all these concrete facts must be established. But Fox would not soon forget the impassioned outburst of Midshipman Gruber, saying things about Fox too outrageous even to be recalled to mind, before the president hushed him with what was a most gentle reproof, and all to the accompaniment of snorts from Lymm. Yes, Fox wouldn't soon forget young Gruber, pale and trembling, standing there belting out what amounted to a hymn of praise for Commander Fox.

How noticeable it had been that Lord Lymm had steered very small after the course of the proceedings had taken their dramatic turn!

The strangest thing of all, of course, was the way in which Fox had been tackling these proceedings on their own terms. He had scarcely thought of a very natural desire to sink his fist wrist deep into the guts of Lymm. He had hardly been aware of that killing rage to rend and smash. He had spoken up when ordered, had kept quiet when ordered, and he had acted as the gallant and upright sea officer.

Well...

Well, it appeared to have paid off, so far ...

Here was the red-coated marine at the door, telling them the court was reconvening. Purvis dashed a hand across his forehead, tugged his jacket straight, hitched his sword, and glanced at Fox.

Fox followed out, and, despite all, he felt the old familiar hollowness between belly and backbone.

The light through those great stern windows had now slanted so that he could hardly make out the faces of the captains at their long table. The clerk was fussing with his papers, as usual. The Deputy Judge Advocate kept swallowing as though he had a quid he could not remove. The blue and gold and white gleamed and twinkled in the cabin.

The flies still buzzed.

Fox stood to the side of his chair, set before the table, his hands at his sides. He felt not so much cold as congealed.

The president cleared his throat.

What he said hardly penetrated to Fox.

How marvellous that curved sword looked!

What a beautiful sight, that curved blade, that stirrup-hilt, the blue and gold sword knot dangling in glory in the sunbeams! What a perfectly delightful sword to own, that naval arm fashioned on the Light Cavalry sword of 1796!

The hilt of that fascinating sword was held out toward George Abercrombie Fox.

Tompkins did not make a meal of it.

There was nothing here of speeches, of remarks about defiant fights to the death, of keeping the flag flying until the ship foundered, of being a credit to the Navy. But, at least, Tompkins had the grace to speak up, at the end, with a covert glance at the slumped and glowering form of Lord Lymm.

"The court is of the opinion," Tompkins was saying, speaking a little more rapidly than usual, "that Commander Fox . . . of His Majesty's late gun vessel *Minion* . . . and the ship's company of the said vessel . . . did use every possible endeavor and exertion . . . and do honorably acquit them ... and they are hereby acquitted accordingly. . . ."

Fox quite felt a shock when Tompkins ceased and that expected: "And may God have mercy on their souls," did not roll out.

Of course! He had been found not guilty! He'd not been found out!

Fox took a grip on himself.

The court was breaking up amid a buzz of voices that drowned out the flies.

Lord Lymm left immediately.

Fox did not bother to watch him go.

He knew he'd not heard the last of that monkey, not by a long chalk. Well, there was Toady Stone and there was Lord Lymm. As enemies, they'd be enough to be getting along with.

Here was Commander Purvis busily buckling on that wonderful sword. The sword belonged to Lieutenant Johnson, second of *Pike*. What an extraordinarily fine fellow was Johnson!

Jack Blane was wringing his hand.

"Congratulations, sir! I knew you had nothing to fear, nothing at all! Why, lay me horizontal, only an idiot could have supposed you guilty!"

"Thank you, Mr. Blane." Fox managed to find his feet in the golden haze. Somehow, this had been an entirely different court-martial from, say, that one in Port Mahon. "I owe you a debt, Mr. Blane, for all your help. Your report was fulsome, sir—"

"Not at all, sir! Not at all! The way you handled *Alouette*—why, I swear, Commander Fox, you could make a ship dance a gavotte if there was a band handy, damn if I don't."

And Lieutenant Jack Blane's ruddy face glowed with his excited admiration. Or, considered GAF getting back to a more normal frame of mind for George Abercrombie Fox, as pleased as Punch at getting a cunning whack in against that bastard Lord Lymm.

The great aft cabin was at once emptying and filling as Fox's court-martial, being finished, gave way to the new court-martial. Fox had heard this concerned an unfortunate midshipman—a man of thirty or so—who had struck out at a lieutenant on being tipped out of his hammock together with the doxy sharing it with him. The midshipman was thirty years old; the lieutenant a mere twenty-one.

That reminded Fox of Kinglake, with the fair hair and the hard-edged features, like those a carpenter might chisel from a block of oak, and that intensely pale face. Yes, an intense man, for all the corn-gold of his hair, was Captain Kinglake. He had been made post in 1795, and now, a post captain with two epaulets and five years' seniority, did carry two years' seniority over Captain Lord Lymm. How many years would he carry over Fox—always assuming that Fox ever did reach the exalted heights of post rank?

Commander Purvis and Lieutenant Jack

Blane were burbling away, clearly gratified by the outcome of the court-martial. Fox's crew were already being shipped off to *Pike*. The warrant and standing officers would be found fresh berths. Fox considered that he could look with a little equanimity on his hands serving under Commander Purvis. The short stout man was a sea officer, and he had shown himself of generous spirit. Truly, G. A. fox was becoming maudlin!

So that the many things that had now to be done could be done with a frame of mind at once at ease—he had been honorably acquitted—and wracked with the most excruciating apprehensions for the future—would my lords commissioners of the Admiralty ever wish to employ him again? Maybe he would at last be tagged with the label of unsuitable, of a man who was a troublemaker, a man too high and mighty, too hoity-toity, ever to be trusted to serve faithfully again.

This evil was known.

Why were there captains languishing on half pay, when others were given ship after ship?

There were always plenty of officers in the Service, far too many, at times, when there were never ever enough men.

After his court-martial at Port Mahon he'd gone straight away to be first lieutenant in Captain Staunton's *Furieuse*. Well, Staunton was now Lord Smithgate, Earl of Brinkhampton, and poor old *Furieuse*'s bottom had fallen out; old Furry-arse would never sail again, and it was highly unlikely that the new Lord Smithgate would, either.

This time, Fox was on the beach, on half-pay, and desperately ready to take what was offered in the way of a vessel. There were very many keen young commanders, queuing up, ready to be handed tidy crisp commands, waiting to shift their swabs from left to right shoulders, to be posted. Fox was a very small fish indeed in an almighty big and hostile pond.

George Abercrombie contemplated his future with surly cynicism tempered by that bitter obduracy that had brought him through, neck and crop, before.

One of the oddest moments of that busy time was seeing young Gruber so close to tears his thin freckled face appeared swollen and bursting with the effort to hold himself in.

"I've come to—to say goodbye, sir."

Fox had to put on a little of the old bluster, the bluffness. He could not allow himself to see the tremble of the lower lip, the rigidity of Gruber's back, the hands gripped into white fists at his sides.

"Goodbye, is it, Mr. Gruber? And where away are you bound, then?"

"Please, sir, I have to go home." Gruber swallowed, a difficult operation in his present condition. "I had hoped, sir, hoped—"

"Well? Spit it out, Mr. Gruber!"

"I will," said Mr. Midshipman Gruber with a sudden rush of recklessness, "give your best regards to Captain Staunton, sir, if you wish–"

"Captain Staunton asked me to keep an eye on you, young man." Fox couldn't unbend now. "Are your books written up? Have you your certificates safe?" Fox had had to go through the tiresome business of fresh certificates, all very legal and fusty and yet highly necessary. Without his papers a midshipman could rot.

"Yes, sir, thank you, sir."

"Well, cut along, Mr. Gruber." As the midshipman made a hesitant beginning to move off, Fox, despite himself, added: "It was good to have you aboard, Mr. Gruber. Maybe someone will make a sailor of you yet."

The navy was a highly technical service. The officers and men used words of exotic flavors, quite incomprehensible to landsmen. Gruber was shaping up nicely and Fox was aware of that old familiar pang at the sight of promising officers and tough fighting men being shipped off in other captains' vessels.

"Yes, sir, thank you, sir," said Gruber again.

His Interest came, however Fox might puzzle over it, from Captain Percy Staunton whose Interest in turn had been looked after by his uncle, Admiral Staunton. That formidable figure would now no doubt feel less concern over a nephew who had become the chief, had become Lord Smithgate. Gruber might do so very well that he, along with all the others, might be posted long before Fox got even a sniff of a hint of shifting his swab. But Fox couldn't really grudge Gruber. Oh, he grudged him, all right, as he grudged Staunton himself, and Lionel Grey, too. But there were some officers whom it was vitally necessary to post just as early as humanly possible. Nelson had been such a one. God knows what shape the navy would be in now if Nelson hadn't been a captain and a commodore at vital moments of action.

In the end Fox had fairly to chase Gruber off.

For some reason the youngster fancied he wished to remain and serve again with Commander Fox.

Fox could not belt out a harsh: "I'll be lucky to get a fodder scow after this, Mr. Gruber!" But he managed to convey some of his starchy philosophy to the midshipman in as tactful a way as he could. Protesting his undying gratitude for what Fox had done for him—Fox kept a straight face—Gruber took himself off.

Fox rolled off to the tavern. He had chosen again to frequent a place somewhat away from the waterfront and dockyard areas, as he often did, and so, clad in his old uniform, that atrocity of a hat upon his head, and with a few coins to jingle in his otherwise empty pocket, he trundled into the *Stag and Hounds*. That, alone, proclaimed the difference. *The Stag and Hounds.* Usually it was something like *The Jolly Tar*, or *The Crown and Anchor* or *The Benbow.*

He took a pint of the tavern's black beer to a side table, beneath a window and thus in something of a shadow from the sill, and sat down and stretched out his legs and sighed, and took a whole pigging swallow. He wiped the back of his hand across his lips, and stared up into the pale eyes and pale face of Captain Kinglake.

"Please do not rise, Commander Fox."

Fox had made no move to do any such thing; but if Kinglake noticed that lack of respect he made no comment. He slid on to the settee opposite Fox's, and placed his glass of brandy upon the polished oak.

Fox said nothing.

He knew that Kinglake must have followed him here. He'd come to this place to get away from the eternal sights and sounds and smells of ships and sailors; what the hell did this icy cold Kinglake want, snooping around and following him?

"May I offer you my congratulations on your acquittal, Commander Fox? It was most thoroughly deserved, I assure you." Kinglake lifted the brandy and twirled it, and from him that was an over-life-sized gesture. "The thing was carried to farcical extremes. The court-martial was a mere formality."

"But it didn't turn out like that."

Fox made no pretence of noticing the difference in their ranks. He'd had this imp up on First Lieutenant's report, and seen his backside tanned across a gun. Now that fair-haired imp was a fully-fledged post captain commanding a thirty-two-gun frigate Fox would have given his eye teeth for.

Kinglake drank, slowly, not tossing the brandy off, and not taking those slatey eyes off Fox, either. Even so, and without any ridiculous notions, Fox knew his own eyes were far more cold and terrible than this Kinglake's. He wondered what sort of captain he'd turned into, and suspected him to be firm and fair, in the better tradition, if the judgement Fox had formed of him as a midshipman was anything to go by.

"You probably wonder why I followed you here, Commander Fox."

"No."

That didn't shake Kinglake. He did not smile. "I think you realize that I was able to afford you some assistance during the court-martial—"

"I do." Fox's words cracked out, low-voiced, flat, spiteful, like the nasty bark of a four-pounder. "For that I thank you, Captain Kinglake." Then, he found himself adding: "But for the life of me I don't know why."

Now Kinglake did smile, and the transformation in that icy face revealed a miracle. He became human, on a sudden.

"You owe me no gratitude, Commander Fox. I remember you from *Invulnerable*, as I am sure you remember me."

Fox did not reply. Caution—caution—*something* was in the wind.

"You will recall our captain during that commission was Captain Cloughton, now Admiral Cloughton."

"Black Dick Cloughton. Aye."

"You had the good fortune, Commander Fox, to be first to Captain Staunton during Cloughton's Action. The Admiral has seen fit to take me into his confidence over certain activities of that action."

Fox wondered just how much Black Dick Cloughton had seen fit to tell Kinglake. Had he told him that Cloughton himself had been incapacitated by his malady aggravated by reckless drinking? Had he told him that Captain Percy Staunton was less than perfect as the captain of an eighty gun ship of the line? Had he told him that it was Fox who had commanded the whole squadron during the action, and had seen off two of the enemy, had blown up two and had captured the remaining three, and all with four ships of the line of generally lesser force? Fox knew that Cloughton was aware of a great deal of the truth, for our Percy had been insistent—glowingly insistent—on telling the admiral for the report. The letter in the gazette had been of quite surprising warmth and value. Perhaps Black Dick had not pushed Fox aside with the command of *Minion.*

Again Fox remained silent. Let your opponent open his guard, do not give him an advantage by a too-precipitous onslaught—Fox knew the theory—but how he would have loved to have brayed out some jocular remark about a drunk and a nincompoop having to be wet-nursed in action!

"The Admiral directs me to acquaint you with his wishes, Commander Fox. He is sensible of past obligations. There is a certain duty you can perform that will stand you in good stead for the future."

"Yes?"

"Yes, Commander Fox. You are aware that Captain Lymm was ordered to—" and here Kinglake actually looked around the low-beamed tavern room with half a dozen men idly drinking across the empty fireplace "—attack Point Avenglas."

"I was subsequently aware of that. At the time I did not know."

"I understand. The man is a fool—" And then Kinglake shut up, and pushed back on the settee, and offered to buy Fox another drink, an offer Fox seldom refused. When he was seated again, Kinglake said: "I have been on an extended cruise, to India, and have but recently returned. I was not on hand during these events. But the Admiral has fully acquainted me with the situation."

"Point Avenglas," said Fox. "What is so special about the place? It's just a wide bay and an inlet—I believe the forts at the mouth have ten forty-two-pounders apiece."

Kinglake's icy manner was thawing. He actually chuckled. Maybe it was the brandy. "Black Dick said you had the whole world's charts in that skull of yours, Commander."

There was no need for a reply to that. Even if it was true—as it very nearly was, bigod!

"Precisely. Lymm's attack failed miserably. There is a quantity of shipping in the inlet. It's bottled up now; but we are forced to maintain a close blockade, which is damned inconvenient. Black Dick has the services of this Frency spy, Etienne. He can get in there. But the Admiral requires the skilled appreciation of a naval officer—"

"I—see," said G. A. Fox.

"Ah—yes. Black Dick would like you to spy out Point Avenglas for him, for he has been given the command. It will have to be done very fast, Commander Fox. Well? What is your answer?"

Chapter Five

George Abercrombie Fox once more stood upon the ground that had nurtured the men who had won so gloriously on the fourteenth of June, this year, battling when all seemed lost to secure the brilliant victory of Marengo.

General Desaix had been shot dead in leading the final attack that had secured the day. The battle had been lost; but there had been time to win another.

"You're a fine plucked lot, Etienne," said Fox as he and the French spy moved into the moon-shadowed darkness of the cliffs. The boat that had brought them vanished out to sea. Out there a saucy cutter commanded by a nineteen-year-old lieutenant would wait just over the horizon, tacking up and down, and tomorrow night would slide in silently again to take them off. If the victor of Marengo had not grasped them in his claws.

To be sure Fox had given this young lieutenant a good hard stare, and he had been fully conscious that his own evil eyes had been a rich ripe green, green as peas. The whipper snapper, Lieutenant Jonathan Algernon Mattison, RN—no less—had stood comfortably on his own deck, in his own vessel, in command, captain of His Britannic Majesty's armed cutter *Daisy*. Even a cutter for a command seemed a grand thing then to Commander Fox, without a ship, without prospects apart from being taken up by a customs patrol of Bonapartistes and having his head blown off against a wall.

"Quiet, my friend," said Etienne, barely whispering. "As they say in the best dramas—the night has ears."

Fox might have said: "I hope the night's damned eyeballs are better than mine." But no one knew of that confounded eye infirmity of his. He slipped on the stones and then at once moved in absolute silence. As a boy he had stalked and slain Red Indians in America. He wouldn't make a noise going ashore on a beach in Bonaparte's France and scrambling up to the cliff top.

A few high clouds drifted across the stars, invisible except for the occultations they caused; the moon would be rising more fully soon, and they had to be in position to spy before that.

Black Dick Cloughton had been explicit.

"I want to know all details of the Point Avenglas fortifications, Commander. Etienne knows the land. You will know the forts and the shipping in the roads."

"Aye aye, sir," Fox had said. And there had been no word between these two, between the admiral and the commander, about just why it was necessary for the inlet and roadstead to be thus surveyed after an attack upon them, and why it happened that it should be this particular commander who had been singled out for this desperate and dangerous work.

Young Kellerman had led a brave cavalry charge at Marengo, and Desaix had brought his division up, and the Austrians had been tumbled into ruin. The French always won on land. Well—almost always. A thin and evil twitch moved Fox's lips by a hairsbreadth. Bonaparte had come a cropper when he tried to take Acre. A handful of British tars and a gang of scroundrelly Turkish irregulars had held him off, licked him and his vaunted veterans, sent him packing with his tail trailing miserably between his legs. Now, of course, Bonaparte had manipulated the gullible French and was now First Consul with immense powers. Fox never could understand, with his tough British phlegm, just how the volatile and excitable and incredibly brave French could have been taken in by the Corsican bandit.

Mind you, the French were a pretty dour lot up in this northern part of the country. Fox was not fool enough to imagine that all Frenchmen were alike, conforming to some mythical pattern held only in an insular Englishman's mind. They hadn't had the same advantages in racial interbreeding as the British, of course; the Normans had remained stagnant, whereas those bastard conquering Normans had been civilized by the Anglo-Saxons, and the Northmen had given a different tinge to England—the whole country was a melting pot. From an alloy came a far tougher metal. Etienne was signalling and Fox checked and looked down.

In that instant he heard the low voices. He could hear, over the slurring susurrations of the waves dragging the shingle on the beach, footfalls and the occasional clink of metal. That metal, in this day and this place, would be fashioned into guns or swords; not into ploughshares.

The two spies remained silent and motionless until the patrol passed. Etienne went to move on. Fox checked him, and waited another five minutes. Then he moved on.

Hitching his folding writing board up by its strap over his right shoulder—the awkward thing hung at an angle and insisted on tangling itself up with the cutlass he had chosen to wear—Fox rose and looked about in the darkling light, and then nodded. Etienne pushed on up the slope of the cliffs and Fox followed. They had lost time. The moon would be up with enough light to betray them by the time they reached the coign of vantage Etienne had promised would afford them the best panorama. Fox bashed his feet down hard and dug into the springy turf, hustling Etienne.

"*Corbleu,* M'sieu Fox! You are made of iron!"

"Don't forget it, Etienne."

"We are almost there. That knoll there, see . . ."

Etienne pointed. Fox could just make out the rounded knoll looming up in the dimness, a dome rising from the edge of the turf-covered cliff. Beyond that lay a sheer drop and the end of the bay, and the beginning of the inlet. From there, a spy could do useful work.

Etienne would have gone on and around the knoll, pushing on at the same speed, his head down. Fox again halted him. With his thin lips pressed against Etienne's ear, below the old tricorne the Frenchman wore, Fox said: "You'd run right on to a caltrop, Etienne, me old sport. Bide awhile until I scout the place. Boney keeps his vedettes on their toes."

Etienne did not laugh; but his harsh exhalation of breath was tantamount to a guffaw of amusement.

"You speak, George, always, as though you and the archcriminal Bonaparte are locked in a personal battle."

The idea filled Fox with an amusement he had no wish to share.

"I've dotted his 'i' for him once. I robbed

him of a battery he was in sore need of. Now wait—quiet."

Fox moved away with that silentness that always startled those unaccustomed to his ways.

He went around the side of the knoll with the moon beginning to bloom and turn a reddish-silver light upon the close-cropped turf. The far side of the knoll revealed no waiting sentry, and Fox turned. He couldn't make out the form of Etienne clearly; but he knew the spy could see him, so he waved, beckoning. Etienne came on. Together they moved around the last segment of the knoll. Here a chalky path no more than a foot's width across led down, puddled here and there, along the cliff edge. The sheer drop sucked at them from their right side. Beyond lay the inlet and the distant tangle of shipping, almost impossible to discern apart from a tangling mass of lines in the dimness. Here Fox fancied he might see what was truly there better than Etienne, for all the spy's good eyesight.

The little path broadened at its lowest dip, before it rose again, still skirting the sheer drop, and so wended on across the cliff. At this broad part—and that broadness was not above a foot in width—a black hole revealed a hollow in the knoll. That knoll shielded the burrow from observation from the landward side, the rising path obstructed any views along the cliff edge. Directly facing the entrance to the burrow where the path broadened slightly grew a straggly clump of gorse. Fox nodded.

"I'll allow you know your own country capitally, my dear Etienne. You couldn't want a better spy hole."

"It brings back memories, George." Etienne called him George now with a free familiarity. Not as Marianne had called him George, naturally. Sometimes the M'sieu Fox would slip out, and then Fox paid extra attention.

"Let's get ourselves stuffed in, then, Etienne. We have all day tomorrow to observe. We don't want to be picked off like a couple of coneys by another night patrol."

The burrow was about three feet high and extended some way into the chalk of the knoll, before narrowing and dipping down. Fox saw no rabbits. The chalk struck chill to his hand. He unslung the map case and the writing board and stacked them neatly to one side. Etienne took out his two double-barreled pistols and placed them on the chalk. It was very dark inside the burrow, they could only lie there, side by side. Fox took out his own two double-barreled pistols. He could feel them, even if the starshine and moonlight were nowhere near strong enough for him to see them.

In that dimness Fox began to load the weapons.

Etienne heard him, and put his face down, looking, his hands out, feeling.

"*Parbleu*, George! You landed with empty pistols?"

"They'd have been useless had they been loaded, Etienne. That sparky young midshipman let far too much water slop inboard and their allowance of spray was enough to make a fourteen-ouncer turn green."

"I understand—but! Suppose we had been met on the beach by a patrol? What then? *Hein*?"

"Rush 'em with the cutlass. A pistol would have got in the way. It was dark."

Etienne shook his head—Fox did not see the gesture but he heard Etienne's neckcloth rustling. "You are indeed an odd man, my friend."

It did not seem odd at all to Fox, merely common sense.

Fox had carried the telescope in its leather case slung around his neck and Etienne had carried the knapsack with their rations. Feeling peckish, both men gnawed away at heels of bread and cheese, chewing thoughtfully, masticating carefully, for Fox's teeth, although in remarkably good condition were also in no condition to be abused and he guessed Etienne's were likewise, and, between mouthfuls, exchanging a few low words.

The night passed. They dozed from time to time; but Fox with the caution of a lifetime of excursions and alarms made sure both did not doze at the same time.

With the dawn they stirred and stretched and blinked and settled down for the serious business of the day.

As the sun circled so the light would strike into the inlet at different angles bringing out differing facets of the scene spread below in light and shade. Fox got to work at once.

Any distaste the simpletons of the Service might feel for the duties of a spy simply could not touch Fox. He knew of men who had indignantly refused even to talk with a man who had come in from the enemy, with valuable information, on the grounds that such conduct was not that of a gentleman.

Gentleman! Fox had very little time for cretins like that.

This was war. No one liked it—again except for those blood-thirsty maniacs who always thrive in wartime, finding in legalized murder bloody outlets for their own sadism and sicknesses—but if old England was not to be crushed beneath the tyrant's heel, every effort must be made. And Fox believed passionately—for he had seen, he had seen!—that the tyrant would indeed crush down very hard on Albion's Isle. There'd be no mercy from the conqueror. If England failed to win this war, it would be the end for her. Fox had no love at all for the traditional values Englishmen were supposed to be fighting for. He had seen enough of the poverty and misery of the ordinary people to know that those fat-gutted lords and ladies didn't care tuppence for the common folk. But, all the same, England was still England, and there was still a chance that her institutions would flower into a fairer crop than what was going on on the continent right now.

So, rather bemused but with an iron resolve that intended to look out always for Fox as Number One, he went to work.

As he surveyed the shipping down there, and looked over at the fort on the far side, the one on this side being sited further inland and out of his field of view, he became at once aware of just how ticklish this was, and why that oaf Lord Lymm had failed so miserably.

The light lay mellow and golden across the white cliffs, browned and fissured here and there. The turf glowed a last brilliant green before the onset of autumn, dotted with purple and gold, and the shadows of high clouds moved in gray silent rapidity across the scene. Gulls set up a racket, swooping and diving, and the air held that bracing tartness off the sea.

Fox dipped his pen and drew with a firm hand the outlines of the bay and inlet, checking every now and then through the telescope. He disliked that simpleton's description of a glass as a "bring 'um near" but it was certainly doing that now.

As a draughtsman Fox was perfectly capable of setting down details of a fortification, an anchorage, the street pattern of the town. The Navy possessed a surprisingly large number of gifted officers who could really draw and paint, water-colorists of high caliber. Fox did not pretend to join their ranks. But he could produce a sketch plan that would give all the details in absolute clarity an attacking force would need to know on the night of the onslaught.

The activity of a seaport town went on as the day lengthened. It could not rightfully be termed the normal activity, for while a few small fishing craft pushed off to set their nets in the bay, there was no great exodus of vessels to net the sea beyond. Out there a squadron of the Royal Navy lay on guard. Of course, fishing vessels did put out, the lobster pot men among others, and they would not in general be too molested, for they might bring information as well as lobsters and fish. But a more rigid frame of defence had been clamped down on Point Avenglas. Fox watched the activity, and made meticulous notes, and stared through the spyglass, and added to his sketch plan as more and more detail became visible.

"How many warships are there, George?"

Fox lowered the glass and rubbed his eye.

Well, that was the nub of the operation, of course.

"If you don't count the rowing gun

boats—and they'll be there, all right, although hidden from our view—there lies the main force. Two damn great forty-fours." Fox rubbed the doeskin cloth thoughtfully across the lens. "And there are three sloops—corvettes—and a gaggle of smaller craft. And, also—here, look."

Etienne took the glass and stared when Fox directed.

"But she is sunk, George!"

"Aye. She's sunk all right."

Fox took the glass and once more rested his elbows on the chalk—and what that was doing to his blue uniform he wouldn't care to think—and focused the glass upon the hulk.

She lay athwart the main channel, so that no vessel might enter directly but would have to go round her bows or stern. She had been a seventy-gun ship, one of the old fashion, but now her masts had gone, much of her poop had vanished, a few huts sprouted uglily along her deck. She was a sunken battery, a block ship, no doubt reinforced with tough oaken baulks. She was a veritable fort, stuck there across the mouth of the inlet, denying easy access to anything coming up the bay.

"They'll have put forty-two-pounders into her lower gun deck. And, at a guess, twenty-fours on the upper." Fox let the glass droop. "She's a mighty tough nut to crack, wedged there in the jaws of the inlet. No wonder that oaf Lymm didn't break through."

"She will never sail again, George."

"She don't damn well need to, Etienne! Bigod! She's like a bloody great iron lid clapped on a cauldron. It'd take a vessel of great force to smash past her, and no liner will get into the bay on a tack to take her past without being raked to hell and gone. H'mm. Black Dick Cloughton will cough fit to bring up his ring when he hears about this."

No ideas of sympathy for Lymm entered Fox's flinty heart; but he could see that an officer charged with the attack, with gun-vessels, would come sorely adrift. The French would have soldiers in the block-ship, too, ready to repel any attempt at boarding.

"Point Avenglas turns out to be a hornet's nest."

This Etienne was a Frenchman and a very brave man. He had been born in these parts and had gone to Paris where he had acquired speech patterns he could employ when necessary; what he had done there, what his past history was, remained unspoken between them. But Fox quite clearly caught the underlying hopelessness in Etienne. His country had been ravished by the Revolution and now was being exploited and gulled by the Corsican Bandit; Etienne would go on fighting but he was more easily discouraged than

Fox liked, for all that Fox had already had proofs of Etienne's courage.

"Hornet's nests can be smoked out, Etienne." Fox half-turned his head in the slanted shadow of the burrow. He had to give this man a little of his own strength, or, rather, to show Etienne the way back to his own strength. "We're two very small items in the greater affairs of state. Why, that Boney's probably prancing around at Malmaison now, wondering who's tumbling his black-fanged Josephine, wondering which of the generals' wives he'll invite for supper and wine tonight—but I bet the cunning bastard knows all his regiments, every one, and he'll know all his gunners, too, and his strong points. But I remain to be convinced he knows the difference between a jib-boom and a spanker."

"*Hélas,*" said Etienne, breaking a chunk off the remains of the bread. "You are right, *mon ami*; and yet I sorrow for my poor country. Will we ever rid her of that depicable Corsican Bandit?"

"Take it from me," said George Abercrombie Fox. "The man hasn't been breeched yet who can get the better of old England."

So it was cheap rhetoric; perhaps it was downright unkind in the eyes of a Frenchman concerned over his country; but it was damned true and it was one of the guiding lights of Fox's existence. Only one. The most important guiding lights, as ever, were a careful consideration for his own skin, a fanatical determination to do whatever was necessary for his family of Foxes down by the Thames, and after that to look out for the tiny handful of people he thought of as—if not friends—then good companions.

Practical matters obtruded then—as though the preceding thoughts were not the most important and practical matters in his entire life!—and Fox swung the spyglass up again. He was careful to slip the leather tube over the lens so that no sun glitter would sparkle back to watchful eyes on any of the ships, or on the ramparts of the fort, and so betray them.

People were moving about down there, busy on the errands of the day. Despite that activity, clearly apparent to Fox, lay a kind of senility upon the town and the shipping. They were mewed up here. A glaciation of inertia possessed everything below. A company of soldiers marched off to the fort, their blue tailed coats and white breeches making a fine sight with the sunglint off their muskets. A drummer lad marched along and faintly across the water, the stirring rat-tat-tat reached up to the cliffs, making the sea birds wheel and cry, making Fox once more consign to the blackest of hells all military organizations that employed young boys in the thick of the fight.

The day wore on.

The supposition Fox came to was that

Lymm's attack carried out at night and with all the smoke and darkness and confusion attendant upon that, had failed to reveal any weak point. The presence of the blockship must have been realized, of course, no one was going to miss that. If Fox could not see any easy way around that, past the guns of the blockship and the guns of the fort, on to the guns of the warships moored beyond, then there just was no easy way. He lay there all that golden afternoon, staring at the scene below, figuring and calculating, and in the end always coming back to his instant original conclusion.

Etienne gripped his arm; but Fox had already heard the voices coming up the path along the precipice toward their burrow.

Chapter Six

"Go on, Angelique! You have to, one day. So why not now? With me?"

"With you, Frederic, you lump?"

The girl's light laughing voice, taunting, teasing, floating on the still air, the sunbeams striking across the still water below, the gulls circling and crying, and the lad's voice eager and quick and choked with desire he had only recently come to recognize.

"You know how much—"

"And when you march off to the wars, Frederic, what then?"

"I will never forget you, Angelique. Never!"

They came into view, now, walking slowly along the path. The girl walked in front, her long skirts covered yet by a white apron, her blouse already undone to the first button at her throat, her face and arms glowing and rosy. Her dark hair under her mob-cap hung with just that amount of disarray to proclaim of a scuffle lower down the cliff.

The soldier boy walked after her, as perforce he must on so narrow a trail, his open face, so heartbreakingly young and unlined, filled with all the restrained passion of the untried in chase. Fox saw everything and then looked at his uniform. A dragoon. White breeches, green coat, brass fittings, red epaulets, he looked the real figure of a soldier, even though the color schemes clashed, as they so often did in French uniforms. He wore no hat or helmet. He carried no weapons—well, no weapons suitable for the din and struggle of real battle. He kept putting his hands out to touch the girl and she kept squealing and beating him away, while she climbed down the narrow path toward the burrow.

Fox sighed.

She was well aware of what was going to happen, else she would never have come here in the middle of the afternoon with a soldier boy. She was probably a maid from one of the better houses in the town. Fox wondered just how many soldier boys she had brought here, and seen off, and never seen again, their bodies moldering on the glorious Corsican's even more glorious blood-soaked battlefields.

With the barest whisper of breath, Etienne said: "They are coming here, *corbleu*, here!"

"Whatever they think they are going to do," said GAF with acerbity, "will not turn out as they expect."

The two spies remained concealed in the

shadows of the burrow. The girl and the dragoon ran down the last few steps into the slight widening of the path and here the dragoon could catch her. She was an old hand at this game. Her nimble fingers unlatched her blouse further, quickly, her fingers and their work hidden from the dragoon. He was breathing so loudly Fox felt he could have let off his pistols and the boy would scarcely have heard them.

"I know what you want, Frederic! You are terrible! But, this time, perhaps, I shall be kind to you."

As she had many and many a time before, so Fox considered, watching with the interest of the old hand.

Angelique freed the last fastening of the front of her blouse, still hidden from the dragoon. His uniform was just that much too big for him. His boots were highly polished and already the chalk showed dustily upon them. He wore no spurs. He was just a trooper, probably his number was still wet.

The girl ripped her blouse open and Fox took full advantage of the view. Then the girl swung about, her arms wide, and Fox saw the boy's jaw drop, the blood rush to his face and then ebb, his eyes pop out. He couldn't speak. He stood there, trembling, his mouth wide open. The girl laughed in that peculiar vixenish way so peculiar to the circumstances.

"Why, Frederic, I believe you've never—"

"Angelique!" He spoke. He jumped forward, his arms going about the girl, his face over her shoulder. His eyes were wide open, staring, unfocused. Fox did not think the boy even saw him as he stood up and, holding the pistol by the butt, brought the double-barrels down on the dragoon's head.

The girl and the boy would have toppled over the cliff if Fox had not caught them with his other hand and savagely wrenched them back from the brink.

They tumbled to the chalk before the mouth of the burrow.

The boy flopped loosely sideways.

The girl sprang up, to her knees, looking about with so much shock evident on her round glowing face that the speed of the attack had not yet registered, and then she tried to run and scream. Etienne caught at her, gripped the loose edges of her opened blouse. The girl ran helter skelter, shrieking. The blouse ripped away in Etienne's fingers. She ran full tilt into Fox, who staggered back, almost going over the cliff. He swore and clapped a hand over her mouth to stop her yelling.

"They could hardly miss hearing her in Point Avenglas!"

Fox held the squirming Angelique. She kicked and struggled and tried to bite. The remnants of her blouse hung down over her skirts. Fox pushed her into the burrow, face down, still gripping her jaw so she couldn't bite.

"A spitfire, this, my friend."

"*Parbleu*! And what a figure!"

Fox had already sized up the neat whiteness of Angelique's breasts, the smoothness of her waist, and felt comment to be superfluous. But then, that was a Frenchman's way.

Speaking a deliberately slurred French of the locality, picked up with his habitual speed during his time in Panterre, Fox said: "If you do not stop this silly yelling I shall hit you on the head—very hard."

She sniffled and sobbed, but she quietened down.

"You would not strike a woman, Geo—"

"If necessary I would strike anyone." Fox twisted the girl over, saying: "If you do not make a sound I will let you up. If you shout—" He let his evil eyes take their toll of her courage; his gaze traveled deliberately along her naked body. Gently, Fox disengaged his hand, ready to slap it back the instant she yelled.

She did not yell. She was panting, and in a moment she might well be crying; but she said: "You have killed Frederic! Murderer!"

"He'll wake up with a headache. But you call us murderers—assassins—we are, oh, yes, we are, when a silly *poulle* pushes her white neck into affairs that do not concern her."

She lay there, panting, her dark eyes looking up with more anger than fear.

"You are not smugglers! I know them all hereabouts."

"We are who we are, Mademoiselle."

She digested that. Fox was intrigued by her apparent lack of fear after the first shock. He had not failed to notice the condition of her nipples, and he surmised that she was a hard-headed, cunning, shrewish little vixen, so well aware of her beauty that she had become accustomed to twisting all the young men around her little finger. She lay back now in a more relaxed pose, making no effort to draw up the rags of her blouse. Etienne had dragged the dragon half-way into the burrow and was busily tying him up with suitable items of his own equipment.

"We shall slit your throat, my girl, as soon as look at you," said Etienne, and jerked a knot tighter.

"That is not what this one wishes to do to me," said Angelique, letting her eyes slide away from Fox's gaze, and she had the effrontery to reach up and smooth her hair.

Fox felt a profound disquiet. Marianne had seen naked lust in his eyes, or so she claimed, and now this slut Angelique said she knew what Fox was thinking. He'd merely given her figure the attention it deserved, noticing what nature had already done to it in anticipation of what the dragoon would very soon do. Was he getting old, then, that he couldn't shut off his lecherous thoughts from shining from his damned ice-floe eyes?

Now Angelique was looking frankly at him.

"You are not smugglers, no, that is so. You wear a uniform of a regiment I do not know—we have had a number here and I know all the soldier boys' brave uniforms. What is your regiment, you assassin, you?"

Etienne said: "He belongs to the Br—" when Fox bellowed and pushed sideways so that Etienne fell across the unconscious Frederic, now bound and gagged.

"*Mon Dieu*! What are you playing at?"

"I do not wish the girl to know how we stand with regard to Bonaparte. You know what they are like here—" Quite deliberately, quite maliciously, Fox spoke French. He wondered if the girl would take the bait and the hook.

The uniform must have convinced Angelique, for she said quickly: "We are all good Bonapartistes here, as well you know!"

"We are not convinced, Angelique."

"So you spy on us to see if we betray the First Consul to the English!" She had seen the telescope, the impedimenta; vixen and young-boy-eater she might be, she was no fool.

Fox sighed. He sighed out loud, a doleful sound that must have convinced the girl he was acting with great sorrow.

"You know how the First Consul detests traitors, Angelique. They try to blow him up. He is a great man, and these miserable villains seek to assassinate him. I think you have seen too much." Fox glanced at Etienne and sighed again, heavily. "There is nothing for it, *Pierre*—we will have to knock these two on the heads and throw them over the cliff."

"Indeed, *Jean*, I think we will."

Angelique shrieked at this and sat up so that she banged her head on the chalky roof. In the ensuing dust and confusion she tried to make a run for it, until Etienne laid a grip about her ankle—a neatly-turned ankle—and dragged her back. Fox gripped her wrists in his hands and pulled her to him. He did not enjoy this play-acting.

"You are a silly girl, Angelique. You would try to ruin Bonaparte's plans!"

"No, no! I never would! Oh, please do not throw me over the cliff!"

"We may have to, if you do not behave yourself."

"I will! I will!"

Fox looked at the still body of the dragoon, his green coat now white with chalk. "Best tie her up and gag her, Pierre. It will be safest. Then we will decide if we will have to throw her over the cliff."

"Let us throw her over now."

Fox decided this had gone on too far. "No. We tie her up. I think she will be a good girl and we will not have to throw her over. We will let her go tonight."

"But I must go back! There is much work to do. Madame Fessard will require her dinner—"

"Madame Fessard, is it?" said Fox. "One wonders how devoutly she shares her loyalty between the First Consul and the Virgin Mary—eh?"

Angelique looked frightened—and Fox noted that with a welling of an emotion he supposed was sorrow. This girl, for all her airs and preenings and seductions of simple soldier boys, had proved herself full of spirit. Two ferocious men dragging her down, and she with her blouse all ripped off! had not cowed her; those few simple words had made a transformation.

"Tie her up and gag her." Fox looked at her white body, with the shadowed bar of the burrow roof upon it, emphasizing the curves. "Be gentle with her, Pierre."

With Angelique safely bundled up and stowed alongside the dragoon, who still lay unconscious but who would soon wake up, Fox could once more turn his mind to the affairs of high importance that had brought him here. He shifted uncomfortably. The girl's eyes watched him, bright, and he wondered at a world that made spying on shipping and forts and soldiers of more consequence than responding to that bright light in a girl's eyes, that made him tie her up and gag her, instead of—

"Something is moving, Geo—Jean. Beyond the town."

With a sigh Fox took up the telescope and peered.

At once he was again the dedicated professional sea officer.

He could not now make the normal remarks he would have made. He had no intention of killing either the dragoon or the girl, and so, intending to let them go, must ensure they knew nothing.

Beyond the town a dun-colored mass, shot through with a blue haze, and above it the twinkle of many bayonets, proclaimed a body of troops on the march. Fox watched. They marched into the town, and as the autumn sunlight sank and the day began to chill, he saw them dispersing. They might be a part of the garrison returning from a route march. They could well be fresh arrivals, reinforcements. He judged there was a good battalion, a demi-brigade, and the presence of baggage carts would seem to confirm the latter supposition.

Bonaparte—or his generals charged with the defense of the coast in these parts—was sensitive, then, about the English force hovering over the horizon. Well, damn 'em, so they should be!

The troops vanished in the streets of the town.

Every musket there could be trained on an attacking force, from the fort, from the block ship, from the shore. A new and sizeable force had been added to the equation.

Shadows grew long over the water and the evening chill came dropping down over the water and the cliffs. The water moved uneasily and gradually took on a more leaden hue. The radiance of the day faded.

Fox pondered the arrival of these troops. This young lad, lying here now, pale, the blood dried on his scalp where Etienne had cleaned it up, what was he doing at Point Avenglas? The boy's eyes had opened, and he lay there, confined in his bonds and the gag, no doubt petrified as to his future. Did he belong to the town? A gallant young soldier home on leave? Or was he one of a strong force of cavalry posted here? With the troops billeted in the houses, and horse lines invisible beyond the far walls, presumably, Fox had no way of judging the numbers involved. His main duty lay with the seaward defenses. But—cavalry? Was a scheme afoot here?

He rolled over and rested the telescope.

Maybe he might use these two poor wights to spread a little discomfiture. If they reported the presence on the cliffs of two men, one in a strange uniform, the other in civilian dress, it was very likely that the information would come to the ears of the authorities, and they might easily guess the truth. A little subterfuge, then, would not come amiss. If something was brewing, Fox had the shrewd idea it would have to do with those two forty-four gun frigates down there, beautiful craft, strong and heavily armed, extremely tough opponents. If they were allowed to sail, they could cause havoc from here to Pondicherry.

The slanting light, now almost gone, opened up a fresh pattern of lights and shades in that tangle of shipping down there. Fox wiped the telescope glass very carefully, rubbed his eye, shut it for a space and then clapped it to the eyepiece.

Down there he had counted the vessels, apportioning them probable tonnages by their rigging. But now he saw that at least one and possibly two could be reasonable-sized vessels, ship-rigged, storeships. He stared intently; but the same infuriating angle of wall down there prevented a close observation of the hulls. Well, he knew his duty and that did not include destroying the whole mission by creeping down the cliff to see better and being apprehended. Cloughton would want to know about the blockship, the way she was moored, the distances involved. All these things Fox had noted down.

So, to the spreading of the word . . .

He caught Etienne's eye, out of the observation of either the dragoon or the girl, and he winked. Such a gesture for Fox smacked of the vulgar; but as the most vulgar of vulgarians, he supposed, it suited.

"Pierre," he began, speaking in a low voice, but a voice of a lowness calculated to travel easily to the listening ears of Frederic and Angelique. "The *mitrailleur* of Lyon will be most pleased with our report. And if General Vandel puts the case cleverly enough—"

"Oh, him," put in Etienne, catching on quickly and playing up. "He is an old fogey; but he has no love of Jacobins, and Fouché will no doubt treat him as he deserves."

"Joseph Fouché," said Fox, letting the words roll around his mouth. "Joseph Fouché. I trust the good people of Point Avenglas have not been acting foolishly."

At the first mention of the *mitrailleur* of Lyon, Joseph Fouché, Minister of Police to Bonaparte, first citizen, the eyes of the two prisoners widened. They both lay rigidly still.

Fox felt some satisfaction that, by now, the story that two of Fouché's dreaded agents had been keeping an eye on Point Avenglas would be more readily believed than, say, a story that two English spies had been doing that selfsame thing.

Now the shadows had dropped all across the water of the bay and the inlet lay shrouded in darkness, punctuated by a scattering of lights. Etienne moved out of the burrow and stood up.

"*Corbleu!*" he said, stretching. "Now we must go back to Paris and report."

Fox bent to Frederic.

"I will loosen Angelique's bonds—a little. There will be time for you to return."

A shake of the head—well, what did that mean? Fox had no inclination to find out. Etienne turned, a shadow in the early night with the first stars just pricking out over his head. "Make haste, *mon ami*; we have far to travel this night if Fouché is not to be kept waiting.

He walked on up the little narrow path above the cliff.

Fox bent again to the dragoon.

"It is necessary I do this, Frederic." And he hit him again, a more gentle tap, one to put the boy to sleep once more.

Angelique let out a muffled squeak through her gag. Fox ripped off the boy's bonds and then stripped the green dragoon coat off. He rebound the dragoon's wrists. Then he bent over Angelique, the coat swinging in his fist. He looked down on her. Her white skin showed goose-pimples. Deliberately, not a man to waste an opportunity, Fox reached down and stroked first one breast and then the other. She stared back at him, her eyes brilliant. He threw the coat down over her and tucked it in at the sides. "This will keep you warm enough until you break free." He gave a tug to her bonds and loosened them, enough so that a half-hour would see her free. Then, without a look back, all his impedimenta lashed about his squat frame, he went outside into the night.

He'd tried to warm the poor girl up; it would get cold up here very soon.

With his habitual silence he followed Etienne along the narrow chalk track which glimmered palely. He looked up. A loud and hectoring voice broke from the shadows ahead.

"Duval? Frederic Duval? By God, I'll open your tripes for you!"

Fox dropped to a knee. He could see Etienne, stopped on the track, hard edged against the sky. A fresh figure came into view, a dark figure with a dragoon helmet atop a square head. The clink of a saber sounded, then a lantern-light flashed.

"You're in for it now, Duval! I'll see to it you're flogged, degraded, you'll slave for—"

Fox knew the breed. This was a sergeant, setting out to chase Frederic, probably already knowing where the lad had gone and with whom, wanting to get a slice for himself. Slowly, cautiously, Fox began to take out his black silk kerchief.

Etienne said: "Sergeant! I could not help it—"

Fox grunted. That wouldn't fool a tough sergeant of dragoons for a second.

"I gave you long enough. Duval! Now I'm—"

"Please, Sergeant–"

"What?" The change of expression blasted in the night. The sergeant knew this man was not Frederic Duval, trooper in his troop of calvary.

The lantern light flashed. Fox saw Etienne's head abruptly haloed. He saw beyond that, to the big horse pistol in the sergeant's hand. The long muzzle lifted and centered on Etienne. And–more Fox saw. Etienne's own double-barreled pistol was leveled, the barrel gleaming in the light just visible beyond his body. If either man fired that would be a signal shot to the entire garrison! There would be soldiers wanting to know who had fired, alarms would be raised, drums would beat, there's be packs of Boney's men everywhere. Some would be bound to run down to the shingly beach where the boat from *Daisy* was due to touch.

Everything would be ruined!

The black silk kerchief, neatly triangled and folded, held a pistol ball in the center fold. Fox took the corners between his fingers. This, he could still do. He would never forget his days on the marshes with Jake Fox, the way they had to knock their supper out of the sky as it whirred up on wide wings, or go hungry.

"Hold still, there!" The sergeant might be nonplussed for the moment; Fox knew that Etienne would fire in the next second. The sergeant, still unsure, launched into a whole string of foul words and abuses, and it seemed to Fox that Frederic could not lead a very happy life under the orders of this man. The swing whirled.

The ball sped true.

The sergeant let out a startled yell. The lantern flew away and smashed into the chalk, exploding, rivering a small flame until it spluttered out. But the sergeant had toppled the other way. With a long despairing yell he plunged over the cliff.

Well, that had been no part of Fox's intentions.

"*Mon Dieu!*" Etienne swung about. "The poor devil—but he would have been a dead man the next instant, I swear it!"

"Aye—and he may have a troop of his men around. Travel fast, Etienne, and travel quietly!"

They made their way along the cliff edge, and then struck across the turf and so clambered down the cliffs and over the rocks to the shingly beach. They did not speak. What was one dragoon more or less to Boney? Nothing. But that dead soldier might have a mother, a wife, children. Well, so there was a war on—could that excuse what had happened? If Fox had met the man in hand to hand combat on the smoke-wreathed decks of a ship in action, he would have pistoled him or cut him down without a second thought.

Warning: The Surgeon General Has Determined
That Cigarette Smoking Is Dangerous to Your Health.
© Lorillard 1975
Hello
Max.
The maximum
120mm cigarette.
Great tobaccos. Terrific taste.
And a long, lean,
all-white dynamite look.
Menthol or Regular.
"Hello long,
lean and
delicious."
MAX
MENTHOL 120's by KENT
MAX
FILTER 120's by KENT
Regular: 17 mg.
"tar," 1.3 mg.
nicotine; Menthol:
18 mg. "tar," 1.3
mg. nicotine av.
per cigarette by
FTC Method.

Now he had not intended to kill the man, just to knock him out. His shot, then, had not flown true. The sling had not exactly let him down but had not acted in the way Fox wished it to act.

Then he thrust these ugly thoughts from his mind.

In a sty one acted like a pig—otherwise one was trodden on and went nostrils under in the filth.

His shoreside friends, Wordy or Godwin or Sam, for instance, would recoil in horror from the blood upon his hands.

People like Black Dick Cloughton would consider merely that he had done what he was paid to do, what it was his duty as an Englishman in the midst of a horrific war to do.

Actions were looked at in different lights according to the viewpoint of the observer. Fox felt no guilt. He felt hardly any sorrow. The sergeant was—had been—a nasty bastard, after the manner of his kind, that was clear. Maybe Frederic, if he ever knew, might thank him. Boney wouldn't care about the sergeant, that was for sure. But he might care that two spies had wormed their way to half a secret of what was going on in Point Avenglas.

Life was held very cheaply in this day and age, despite the finer feelings of a few poets and philosophers.

There would be very many more deaths before the mad tyrant Bonaparte was dragged down and the world could turn to peace.

Chapter Seven

Nuthatch had served her country well; but now she was past all ideas of glory and of breasting the foaming seas, her canvas all drawing, her forefoot breaking down the green billows and sheeting clouds of spray into the air, her guns run out and ready to belch for their anger. She had been a twenty-four gun sixth rate. Built in 1760 at the Lower Trinity Street yard of the shipbuilding firm of Wells, she was a good honest example of English construction.

Fox stood on the hard stones of the dockside and looked across at *Nuthatch*, and his mind's eye conjured up some of the actions and adventures of her past, and he wondered if he, too, like the ship, was growing old and past it.

Wells had built many fine ships; in 1760, the year of *Nuthatch*, Wells and Stanton had built *Essex*, a sixty-four, the year later Wells had built *Cornwall*, a seventy-four. In 1759 they'd built *Basilisk* and *Mortar*, bombs, both. Yes, the firm of Wells was well known to Fox. Very well known. In the year of his birth, in the gutter opposite Tyburn Tree when his Uncle Abercrombie had been hanged, Wells had built *Invincible*, a seventy-four, down in Rotherhithe. This ship might lie here this quietly in the first rays of the morning sun, with the dockyard about already in full energetic activity, with the smoke rising into the nippy air, the smells of paint and tar and the sea scents all about him; but she carried his mind irresistibly back to the Thames of his childhood. The ship had been five years old when he'd been born; he must have known many of the men who had worked on her.

Her master, a saturnine and long visaged individual with a tic in his right eye, an old-hand, a long-service crab-back called Jarvis, came up, touching his hat.

"Commander Fox. We're getting the last of the workmen out now, sir."

"Very good, Mr. Jarvis. I have to see the Admiral, then I shall come aboard directly. About eleven of the clock here."

Fox thus spoke quite deliberately. He might have said six bells; but he wanted Jarvis to understand that there were other people and other things than seamen and ships. He took great store by that in his warrant officers, did Fox, although he might call forth from them only aspects of their sea lore.

"Aye aye, sir. We'll be ready."

Forcing himself not to spit out: "Cheer up, man!" Fox turned away.

After his report, Cloughton had seen there was but one thing to do, and he had obtained the necessary orders, and *Nuthatch* was the result—*Nuthatch* and a maniacal commander to run her.

The weather had turned chilly, although the sun would burn some of the early mist off, there was no doubt autumn was here. Men wore their coats buttoned up, and earlier on there had even been steam coming from the mouths of the workmen. Fox let a shiver go over his shoulders beneath his brand new coat, and then he straightened those wide thick shoulders and set off for *Alarm.*

Rear-Admiral of the Blue Sir Richard Cloughton, with a fine new watered silk ribbon and a star after the successful Cloughton's Action—which would soon receive another more geographical name, so that Black Dick might not set too great a store by his success, as was the navy way—having taken over the command of the squadron that had failed, had taken his coughs and his drinking into *Alarm*, a small twenty-eight gun frigate. He'd run up his flag and gone aboard, and no doubt the captain and the officers were cussing him to hell and gone. There was no room in a twenty-eight for an admiral.

One of the very first duties—although a

duty he would never regard as such—to be attended with great concern and pleasure had been to go and see Grey. Grey had mended, was fit and well, would have a most beautiful scar to add to his dashing rakehell appearance, and was fretting like a virgin at a wedding that he would not be appointed as first lieutenant in *Nuthatch*. Fox had reassured him.

"As far as it is in my power, Mr. Grey. I will talk to the Admiral." Then, seeing Grey's face with the slash down its paleness, the slash of a sword cut blazing there in the quiet room Grey had taken while he recuperated, not wishing to go home and so leave the center of appointment opportunities, Fox found himself adding: "I would not wish to sail with any other officer as my first lieutenant, Mr. Grey, except Mr. Carker."

"If John was here now!" burst out Grey, animated and hectic with the remains of the fever. "He'd be in here with us, roaring to go!"

"Aye, Mr. Grey, he would. And if he was taken you'd be the second lieutenant."

"So I would, sir, so I would."

Fox did not say: "You don't have to look so smug about it!" But Grey must have seen it in his eyes, for his smile, worming the scar about in a way that was incredibly fetching, summed up all the amused toleration and affection Fox felt he must feel for this tarpaulin commander of his.

Although the good Lord alone knew why . . .

After a considerable amount of tacking and filling, Grey maneuvered the conversation, and then trapped Fox, and so got GAF to accept the offer of a loan to cover a new uniform and the redemption of his five ball sword. Fox had felt a gross fool, all hands and feet; but he could not refuse Grey's offer—particularly when Grey said: "And it would be of peculiar delight to me, sir, if you would also avail yourself of the opportunity to purchase a new hat."

Damn Lionel Grey and Fox's hats!

So—so now, here he was, prancing up to see Admiral Cloughton attired in all the glory of a Commander's full-dress uniform, his five ball sword at his side, his gold-laced hat atop his head, and feeling—and he had to admit this because he could do nothing else—feeling absolutely on top of the world.

The naval outfitter had suggested a beautiful new gilt epaulet, to be affixed in lonely glory to his left shoulder. Fox had grunted, drawing the line at such colossal expenditure, for the bill was being sent to Grey who had means of his own, and had insisted his own old epaulet should be given a polish and be affixed to his new uniform. After all, his epaulet did have some gold in it—he was almost sure of that. It did have, somewhere . . .

The early chill had done nothing to damp his feelings of coming excitements. In this

Fox was not thinking of the excitements of war and violent bloody action; rather he thought of the excitements of a successful conclusion to action and then a posting. As he went aboard *Alarm* and down to the great aft cabin, he looked about the twenty-eight, and he hungered for her. A nice, tight, dainty frigate like this, a post captain's command. Bigod! how he'd run her!

He heard Black Dick Cloughton coughing as he went past the marine sentry and, his hat under his arm, into the cabin. That chill sunlight splashed through the stern windows on to a cabin furnished with taste and discretion. Black Dick had taken up residence here as though he owned the vessel—which, after a fashion, he did, even though the captain, one John Sandeman, would hotly dispute that claim.

Sandeman looked to Fox to be a perfectly ordinary example of a British sea officer; erect, bluff-featured, a little running to fat, and somewhat old to be still in command only of a twenty-eight, as though he had begun his race up the Captain's List a little later in life than was desirable. Fox kept his face granite hard. He hadn't even put his first foot on that ladder.

With Sandeman was Captain Kinglake. His fair hair gleaming, his pale features composed, he nodded his head to Fox. Kinglake had paid off his frigate and was now in the process of commissioning *Hecuba* and bore the responsibility of finding a crew among the manifold other duties laid on a captain at this time.

"Fox, is it?" bellowed Cloughton. "*Commander* Fox, hey?"

Cloughton's engorged face turned scarlet, and he let rip a massive burp, and the thick tears squeezed past his tightly closed eyelids. He sat perched on the edge of a chair, his sagging stomach distending his breeches, his coat shoved back out of the way. On the table near his outstretched hand stood a glass. Never one to be far from a drink, Black Dick Cloughton, even at this time of day. He was killing himself, that was clearly evident.

He wore undress uniform, although, with Black Dick, even when he was dressed to kill in all the glory of full-dress and ribbon and star, he looked like a bulbous scarecrow. Captains Kinglake and Sandeman, also, wore undress.

Fox bent his evil eye on the other occupant of the cabin, Commander Benjamin Dawood. This Dawood looked what he was–a young tearaway. His jaw was habitually set into a dashing line denoting charm and ruthlessness. His blue eyes beaming forth on the world indicated a brain fully conscious of what its owner intended, and, bigod! would do! He had been made a commander after Fox–which was a relief–and he was making it very plain that he was going to be posted damn quick. Fox knew he was extraordinarily brave—he'd led a cutting-out expedition as a lieutenant against great odds, and brought out an armed schooner and a fluyt, thus gaining his promotion—but as to Dawood's efficiency and technical competence, Fox had as yet no reliable means of judging. He supposed the gallant officer knew just about enough to pass his examinations, depended on a first-class master, and let Interest do the rest.

Commander Dawood, also, wore undress.

Fox glared about at these four men, all in undress uniform, and became aware that his own full dress blazed in the cabin.

He felt a popinjay, a dressed-up clown.

What a turn-up! How often and often the situation had been quite the reverse, with Fox looking the bedraggled scarecrow, badly clad, shabby. He had consoled himself that he had looked what he was, a professional fighting sea officer.

Now these others looked the fighting men.

Fox looked the dandy.

And, as was usually the case with George Abercrombie, it was all so damned unfair!

Summoned to the presence of an admiral, any officer's first thought would be to rig himself in full-dress, just to be on the safe side, and particularly when the ship was not at sea. There were exceptions, of course; Fox kept his ugly figurehead still resembling some stone gargoyle, and sat at the table in the chair Captain Sandeman indicated. He saw spread out before Cloughton the sketch map he had prepared in that burrow above Point Avenglas, and heartily wished for the company to get on with the business that brought them here.

Any surprise he might have felt at seeking Kinglake here, when his *Hecuba* would not be ready for sea for a time yet, what with the problems of manning, was banished in the realization that Kinglake was acting as a kind of flag-captain already to Cloughton, that the admiral's flag in a twenty-eight frigate was a merely temporary phenomenon, and that Cloughton would be hoisting his flag in *Hecuba* when she was ready.

This Commander Dawood, now . . . He was a fiery spirit, a young man determined to go far, to hoist his own flag at an early enough age to make it count. He'd been given his promotions at the very earliest legal ages possible; he'd be a post captain so fast Fox would still be leaning over to the left with his own swab.

Cloughton dragged out his huge kerchief and mopped his face and brow. He bellowed a few of his enormous coughs, his face shaking, scarlet and bloated, his pouched eyes screwed up. Then, opening those eyes, he fixed them on Dawood and rapped out: "You understand the business we are about, Commander?"

"Perfectly, sir."

"Humph. This damned blockship. No wonder Lymm came adrift."

"He must have observed the blockship, sir," said Kinglake. These men were professionals, with a chart before them, discussing an action. "His report mentions a very great weight of fire, and yet—"

"The lieutenant in command of the leading boat was killed," put in Captain Sandeman. He spoke mildly. Fox was not deceived. He could hear from above the familiar sounds of a ship going through her regular morning routine, and he judged with that implacable mind of his even as he listened to these men in the cabin. Sandeman ran a tight ship.

"Whatever really happened that night, goddammit," shouted Cloughton. "The fact remains. There are two damn great forty-fours in there, needing to be dealt with. God knows what mischief they'll get up to else."

"There's nothing on that coast to stop them if they do get out," said Kinglake.

There was a tiny silence.

Fox knew what these men were thinking. A handful of gunbrigs, vessels like his poor *Minion*, to interpose themselves between the French frigates and the open sea, even with Lymm's *Meteor* to carry a little long-range punch, would mean a trail of devastated British ships and maimed and drowned British seamen. One or two of the short-range carronades might get in a whack or so, but the massive power of the frigates with their long twenty-four-pounders, their heavy scantlings, their superb sea-keeping qualities, would give the gun-vessels no chance. The only thing to be done was to go in after the frigates.

And the bulky, solid, immensely powerful blockship lay sentinel, like a bulldog at the door.

Fox said: "The French have gun boats patrolling, sir. They're fidgety, mewed up in there."

Cloughton coughed and chuckled, the tears dribbling down his shining scarlet cheeks. "Send a youngster like Jeremiah Coghlan to pick himself up a gunboat!"

They all knew the story. On 26 July this year acting-Lieutenant Jeremiah Coghlan, commanding the ten-gun cutter *Viper*, had taken a boat party of twenty men—there were two other boats but they came up late—to take *Cerbère*, a gun-brig mounting three long twenty-four-pounders and four six-pounders. Coghlan had jumped into a trawl net and become entangled and received a pike wound in his thigh. The attack was beaten off. But they'd simply hauled along the side and tried again—to be beaten off once more. Yet a third time they tried—and this against a vessel with eighty-seven men in her—and this time they smashed their way aboard and carried *Cerbère*, killing six and wounding twenty. Coghlan was wounded twice, and the midshipman with him, Silas Hiscutt Paddon, no less than six times. One seaman was killed and eight wounded. The other two boats then joined and under fire from the batteries they towed out the prize.

"He came from Sir Edward Pellew's squadron, watching Port Louis," grunted Cloughton.

Naked envy in Cloughton's voice alarmed Fox.

"We will contrive it, sir," said Commander Dawood. He, in Fox's view, risked a great deal by saying that just then.

Mr. Coghlan had not served the prescribed time; but, nevertheless, he was confirmed in the rank of lieutenant. That, at least, seemed to Fox the right thing to do. It had never happened to him, and he grudged it fiercely to others; but, when all was said and done, it had been a fine hairbrained scheme and deserved notice and reward.

Thoughts of a similar kind sat in all these men's minds. The Navy was just about the sternest taskmaster in the whole world; but when a brave man performed an outstanding deed of valor, when a great victory was won, why, then, the Navy showed the meaning of gratitude. Cloughton, himself, for instance, sported the magnificent small-sword presented to him by the City of London after his victory; a truly fine example of the cutlers' and the embellishers' arts. The shell was enameled with views of the action—delicate and beautiful work with miniature clouds of smoke, and sails, and sea and sky—nothing like the actuality, of course, but the ships were presentable. On the hilt the City Arms had been picked out in brilliants—not diamonds, for Cloughton was no commander in chief, merely a very junior rear-admiral—and with them the name "Hector", the name of Cloughton's ship. Rather, Percy Staunton's ship, for he had been her captain.

Now Cloughton swilled down a fresh mouthful after a fit of coughing, and thumped the table, and roared out: "And I want none o' this nonsense of 6 July last!"

They all knew to what he referred. Fox did not consider the escapade that night to be nonsense. But he knew precisely what Cloughton meant and, seen from the Admiralty point of view, from the angle of the degree to which orders had been carried out, the affair was something that Fox, while admiring as a man, deplored as a sea officer.

He did not say that he would have done better himself; no one would be fool enough to claim that. The thirty-two gun frigate *Andromeda* with a squadron of small craft had been ordered to destroy four French frigates—*Poursuivante*, forty-four; *Carmagnole*, *Désirée*, *Incorruptible*, all forties. Captain Campbell in command of the corvette *Dart*, thirty guns—another such as *Pike*—had performed cleverly, bluffing his way into Dunkirk. The gun-brigs *Biter* and *Boxer* had done well. They were Wells vessels, like *Nuthatch.* There were cutters and small craft, also, in the *Andromeda* expedition.

Désirée had been brought out, with a great deal of cursing and heaving and blaspheming over the bar, cut out by men from *Dart.* The other three Frenchmen had cut their cables and avoided action—and for why?

Because *Comet*, *Wasp*, *Falcon* and *Rosario* had gone rampaging into the action, ablaze from stem-to-stern, bearing destruction in an awful manner down upon the French.

Fireships!

Oh, they had been handled well enough. Most gallantly they had been conducted, and they had not been abandoned until they were smothered in flames. Commander Thomas Leef and a hand had been wounded in the explosion of *Comet.*

But the French had cut their cables and avoided them. True, a fine forty-gun frigate had been taken and added to the Service; but, still and all, the other three had not burned.

"I want those two bastards in there cut out or burned," said Cloughton, and now he was not coughing. "I don't want them left as a perpetual thorn in our flesh."

Commander Dawood nodded again. "I assure you, sir, we shall not leave until we are certain of our mark."

You speak for youself, thought Fox. Hell!

Going down into action aboard a ship he was going deliberately to set afire! He'd be out of it so fast you wouldn't catch a sight of his breeches.

And, all these commanders . . . He had been surrounded by commanders of late. There were John Edwards, Henry S. Butt, Thomas Leef and James Carthew of those fireships, Patrick Campbell of *Dart*, there were all the commanders of the gun vessels out there with Lymm—there was Dawood here. Fox was like to drown in a sea of commanders, all of them pushing and struggling and grasping at that coveted posting.

Well, maybe, considered Fox with suitable Foxy cunning, well, maybe he'd stay a second or two longer on his blazing quarterdeck. But he wouldn't stay there overlong, bigod, no. He was no damned fool of a hero, willing to go up in flames himself. No sir!

"You command *Firedrake*, Commander Dawood," said Kinglake. "A singularly appropriate name."

"Aye, sir," said Dawood, almost smirking his pleasure. He'd sized up Fox on the instant. Despite the flummery of the new full-dress uniform, Fox's antecedents must have seemed clear to him, and Fox had spoken with his normal tones, not rough-edged, as they were bellowing orders, and not cut-glass in perfect mimicry of the aristocrats, either. That would have cut no ice with Cloughton.

"And *Nuthatch*," said Cloughton.

He coughed then, so that he could not go on. It was left for Dawood, very dashingly and with a laugh that was intended to turn away any insult: "A strange name, sir, very strange, I do declare."

"*Nuthatch,*" said Captain Sandeman in his soft voice. "I daresay you know the bird? A very decent little fellow, the only tree-climber with a blue-grey back. Like the tree-creeper. It is of stocky build, short-tailed, and has a most powerful and pointed beak." Everyone in the cabin was looking at Fox. "The nuthatch has a voice of great power and carrying capacity, one of its calls, most wild, is 'pay-pay-pay.' " Fox was painfully aware of every eye fixed on him. "A blue-backed creeper, with a loud carrying voice," said Captain Sandeman. "Short and stocky." He at last looked away. "With a powerful beak."

Fox could have torn off his ears and stuffed them down his throat.

Cloughton's face was so beetroot red it was touch and go if he exploded in bloody tatters about the cabin. Dawood was looking down at the table, his muscles ridged and white about his mouth, struggling to restrain his enormous laughter. Kinglake studied his fingernails.

"Nuthatch," he said at last in that rapier-like voice. "A small bird not above six inches long, yes. But I believe it is a tool-user, and very skillful, too. It puts a nut in the wedge of a tree and hammers it open with its beak. Also, I understand, it can smash open an oak marble-gall and rake out the grub within."

They'd all been laughing at him; but this Kinglake had given them something else to think of. Why?

Nuthatch.

A singularly appropriate name.

And they'd given Dawood *Firedrake.*

Fox did not move a muscle of his face.

He sat there while Cloughton tossed off another glass, while the chart Fox had drawn from his eyrie was pushed about the table, while the final plans were made and the orders given verbatim. Cloughton finished with: "And I'll have your orders written out fair and sent aboard in time. We sail on the morrow, with the tide. We must proceed with all speed."

"It'll be a question of volunteers," said Kinglake.

"Aye," belched Cloughton. "You are fully manned, Commander Dawood? Good, good, excellent. And you, Commander Fox?"

"I go directly to the receiving ship, sir."

Again they stared at him. Cloughton frowned. He said in that ponderous, portwiney way: "I may tell you, Commander, that I could not in fairness give a command to a man who cannot man his ship."

"I–" began Fox. Captain Sandeman cut him off.

"A fine uniform, sir, does not make a fine commander."

Fox had simply to sit there, stony-faced, and take it.

Chapter Eight

"One hundred pounds or a gold medal and chain in lieu," said George Abercrombie Fox, to himself, half-muttering. "Well, the gold's bound to be brass, so I'll take the hundred. And no mistake." These favours which might be bestowed would go only to the captain of a successful fireship. A fireship that missed its mark, or burned out uselessly, or blew herself up with all on board–they would receive standard navy fare–nothing.

He was about to leave *Alarm* when a midshipman, red of face and protruding of ears, almost falling over his own feet, detained him at the gangway.

"Please, sir, cap'n's compliments, sir, and will you pray step below."

"Very good, youngster," growled G. A. Fox, very much the high and mighty commander, swinging an epaulet. He went back to the cabin and, instead of Captain Sandeman, found Admiral Cloughton.

Black Dick looked up, his eyes like poached eggs that had grown legs and were swimming for dear life, and waving an arm towards a chair, slopped wine, and said: "Take a seat, you young rip. You'll take a glass with me?"

Besides being far too early, it was also far too impolitic to refuse.

Fox took the glass, sat down, and waited.

"Hands, is it, young Fox?"

"Aye, sir. It always is."

The bitterness there was marked and plain.

"What I said remains true, sir! If an officer cannot man his command, then—*out!*"

"But the receiving ship, sir—" Fox would beg for men, he'd go down on his hands and knees, if necessary. Pride was for those captains who did not have to support a penurious family down by the Thames, with new arrivals in the shape of brother's wives, babies and more babies, toppled pell-mell all the time.

"I know the damned receiving ship, young Fox!" Cloughton hitched his small sword up and slapped it down across the table. The thing glittered there in the stern windows' illumination. If Cloughton meant the gesture to mean something, then Fox found he had a tremor of hope. "Heard from Cap'n Staunton lately, Commander?"

"No, sir. Not since he became Lord Smithgate."

"Humph. Well, I have."

There was nothing to say to that, except:

"I trust Captain Staunton is keeping well, sir."

"As well as he ever will barnacled ashore."

Fox remained silent.

"You're a foxy feller, young Fox. We ain't had a talk since–since. You lost *Minion*."

"Yes, sir."

"Hmph. Pity, lad, pity. Oh, I know you were acquitted, honorably let off, all that. But it ain't a good thing, egad, it ain't." Then Cloughton leaned back, and drank, and slapped the empty glass down and burst out with an almighty guffaw. "But you're going to lose *Nuthatch*, young Fox. You're going to lose your ship this time, and no mistake."

"Yes, sir."

"Volunteers, it ought to be. Volunteers. Fireships is a damned dangerous game. Think you can play it?"

"I'll manage, sir. About these hands–"

"Confound your hands, sir! You'd better make sure you have 'em. Volunteers if you can. You know what to do if you don't get enough volunteers."

"No captain is letting his men–"

"I know, I know." Cloughton flipped a sheet of paper across the polished table. "Take this to Cap'n Taplow in the receiving ship. He might uncover a few skeletons, or diseased poxed starvelings, or men with wooden legs for you. If he could fob you off with Widow's Men he would, too, sink me!"

As a Widow's Man was invisible by reason

of never having existed but merely being the device by which pay could be skimmed for selected widows, a manning officer would be happy to distribute them. Fox took the paper. It was an order on the receiving ship for thirty men.

"Thank you, sir. Thirty will be ample."

"You're a liar, young Foxy; but ain't we all. Thirty will have to be enough; work her merchant style if you have to. Volunteers." He reached for the bottle, disdaining the glass. "That's a laugh. No captain's having his men take off and maybe never come back . . ."

As far as George Ambercrombie was concerned, thirty men, with no guns to work, and a one-way passage, were ample.

Cloughton suffered from recurring fits; but they did not stop his drinking. The Admiral was drinking himself to death. Now he leaned forward, balancing the bottle, and glared at Fox with the look a snake must favour a rabbit with in the moments before it strikes.

"*Narcissus* just came in, Fox. You didn't know? I don't advise you to try to poach any of her men from the receiving hulk; Captain Kinglake's got his eyes on them."

"*Narcissus*, sir? Then–"

"She's paying off. I remember Mr. Carker–seventh, wasn't he, in *Hector*? A square solemn-faced feller, as I recall."

"Lieutenant John Carker, sir. He was

brought to the attention of yourself by Captain Staunton—"

"Quick, ain't we, still young Foxy? Now clear off and be ready to warp out on the tide. And if you fail me, Fox, I'll have your tripes for breakfast."

With that Fox withdrew.

To hell with going back to *Nuthatch* now! He'd go straight to the receiving ship no—no, better, find out where the good Carker was and rouse him out. What a miracle! Carker would volunteer to come like a shot. No thought of any other course entered Fox's mind. With Carker as his first lieutenant half his problems would be solved. Grey was really not fit yet, and although he'd be disappointed, it would be better for him to recover fully. Grey pretended he was well enough, though. But, John Carker! What a capital stroke of luck!

He had often grumbled about Interest. He knew the system was rotten. But that was when it applied to other people more fortunate than himself. Cloughton had masked his actions well. He'd called Fox back after the planning meeting, so as not to reveal nakedly Influence at work. Fox had an order for thirty seamen. He'd be lucky, of course, if he got twenty of them. He had been tipped the wink that a first-class officer was available. This was Interest and Influence at work, and because it was working for Fox he considered it capital. Well, he was a human being, also, was he not?

There were plenty of men in the Navy who would have given him an argument on that one, though . . .

The order for the hands had been signed and countersigned by those high and mighty officials whose names must be appended to all such documents. Cloughton had been working ashore on his behalf, also, it seemed. Fox considered. On reflection better to make sure of the hands. Some grasping captain would be along and sweep up all who were there, and Fox needed prime seamen who could hand reef and steer, and they were like snowflakes in hell. Mind you, give him a cruise with a gaggle of nuns and he'd have 'em prime seamen—or seanuns—halfway through, God help 'em.

And if any idiot thought that mere empty bragging, Fox could always point to his sea harem in the old *Maria*.

As always, he almost broke into a cold sweat at the thought of what he'd got up to, swanning around in the Med. Those days had seen silly fat sweaty Sophy, daughter of Lord Kintlesham, too. Only now she was slim and elegant and gorgeous, the Duchess of Bowden, and considered that boor Fox to be the loud-mouthed drunk he was in truth.

Thus thinking Fox took himself off to *Nuthatch*. How strange it was commissioning a ship without guns, with a miniscule crew, and with a stores list that was a caricature of what a properly found ship would ordinarily require.

The technical expertise in constructing a fireship held great and profound joys for Fox. In these kinds of details, a maze of technicalities and arcane lore, he was thoroughly at home. He found with each passing hour that he grew more and more cheerful, idiotically so. His own command, his own ship, he as a commander, as captain—wonderful! Of course, he was going to burn the lot; but, still—wonderful!

Going aboard his vessel to the accompaniment of the bosun's pipe—piped by the Boatswain, Mr. Biggers, in person—he was struck by the untruths he had told Cloughton. He had his standing officers left over, men who went with the ship and had found themselves in the unenviable position of volunteering or being looked at askance, old though they might be. Mr. Jarvis the master's lugubrious face hung over Fox's shoulder as he stepped on to the quarterdeck. All the gangways had been ripped out, supposing the old ship ever had had proper gangways in the modern style. She had been rebuilt in her career at the Royal Dockyards at Deptford, so they must have put gangways in her. Now her decks gaped. Mr. Biggers the boatswain and Mr. Earney, the carpenter, hovered ready for instructions. The gunner, Mr. Jobson, was ashore over a matter of match. Fox frowned. Match was going to be of the utmost importance in what lay ahead.

There were a one-legged cook, a couple of boys, a few hands of sufficient age to be trusted about the ship and who would not be accompanying the ship on her last cruise, no purser, and a sailmaker who had fallen down and bruised his side and was now lying in his hammock in his own cubbyhole below groaning and moaning to himself. That was all.

There would be no marines aboard.

The previous activity as the workmen finished up had no doubt conveyed a sufficient semblance of business to the old ship; but now the workmen had gone *Nuthatch* seemed like a graveyard.

There was nothing else for it. He would have to beg the leave of a boat's crew from the receiving ship. Steady men, old hands who could be trusted to shepherd a parcel of hands and not desert as quickly as they could jump over the side.

The look on Fox's face as he reached this decision caused his watchers to freeze up.

"Carry on, if you please, Mr. Jarvis. I'd be obliged if you'd make ready for the hands—twenty, at least."

"It's good news, sir, that we're to get any hands at all. I was afeared we'd never fill the muster."

"We won't, Mr. Jarvis, we won't. But we'll get enough."

So it was in a shore boat rowed by a couple of lusty women that Commander Fox was pulled out to the receiving hulk.

He just wanted sufficient hands to man his ship and take her out to the squadron off Point Avenglas. After that he would rely on the volunteers. Only a miniscule crew would be necessary to take the old ship into the bay for her final voyage.

All the usual clutter of boats hung around the receiving hulk. The ship looked stolid, hulking, a mess, squat and unlovely. The conditions in her would be horrific. Fox knew all about the diabolical conditions in receiving hulks where men were kept safely locked away until they were shipped out again. A seaman might be taken up in the press and never set foot on the land of his native shores for years on end thereafter, every visit to an English port would see him safely stowed away in a rotting hulk, guarded by trusties and marines, to be whipped up and shipped into a new ship like a mere barrel of salt pork. No wonder the men ran when they could.

Further up a seventy-four was being towed along, her masts already struck, going up to the dry dock. Her crew would have been transferred to the receiving ship, either to wait for her refit or, much more probably, to be shipped out with the first captain with a requisition. Fox touched the outside of his pocket. Paper crackled. Bigod! He, George Abercrombie Fox, had such a requisition. If he could so overawe this Captain Taplow, a task of stunning magnitude, he might even get twenty-five men—twenty-two or -three, at the least.

Fox did not know the seventy-four in her disheveled condition, and then a water hoy passed and he turned away and looked at the receiving ship, calculating.

Captain Taplow received him in his cabin, at first with a courtesy that did not deceive Fox for a moment. Taplow had white hair, and a face graven with lines of disappointment, a black patch over one eye. He was so used to whippersnapper lieutenants coming aboard sniffing after men the presence of a commander would signal to him how penurious was the state of Fox's command.

"Thirty, sir!" he said, when Fox presented the paper. "Thirty! Why, my dear Commander, you might as well ask for diamonds! And a fireship! Volunteers, sir, volunteers, and they won't take kindly to it, I can tell you."

Didn't these idiots understand there was a war on?

"I can talk with the men, sir—"

"Oh, aye, you may talk, Commander. I'll allow that, indeed, you may talk to 'em. I'll flemish down a round dozen for you, Commander Fox. A dozen hands—"

"Hand, reef and steer?"

Taplow pursed up his pinched lips.

"As to that, Commander–you ask for rubies, sir, rubies."

Down on the main deck the men milled about aimlessly, and just what sort of deviltries were going on down there Fox did not wish to know. They'd have the shirt off your back, the breeches off your bottom, and guffaw. Plenty of men were never to get past the receiving ship. A knife in the guts, a savage blow over the head–and all for greed, greed . . .

"You can't touch any o' the prime hands from Captain Kinglake's vessel, Commander. They're all spoken for for *Hecuba.* We've had *Seahorse* come in–and the press brought in a score o' farmers–"

"Farmers are no use, sir."

"They're bodies, Commander Fox. They'll learn."

"I fancy *Nuthatch* will not afford them the time."

"The asylum spared us a few t'other day–"

Fox began to feel a certain queasy desperation. He knew these men, and their quality would never volunteer for anything, let alone a fireship. Once they understood what he was about, they'd vanish below in the cavernous recesses of the hulk. And the word was out. He knew that. They'd all know a mad commander with dreams of quick glory was manning a fireship. They would know, also, that a few of them would be forced to go. They'd make it as difficult as they could.

He would have to make his appeal. After that the ship's corporals and the marines would go in and haul out the unfortunates who weren't smart enough.

Forward a party of men were being conducted down and Fox looked forward in the dim light. A few lanterns hung here and there; but not a port could be opened, even with nets. These men would hack through nets, so close were they to escape.

"They've just come in, Commander. A long cruise. Most of 'em are worn clean out."

From the shadowy shapes Fox could see the men stood or ambled with a dispiritedness that moved him. Men shouldn't have to be treated like this. And yet, what else could be done? If they were given leave they'd run. Leave of absence was sheer lunacy.

"*Gorgon*'s being taken into dry dock, Commander. You probably saw her being towed up. The men have just come aboard."

"*Gorgon?*" said George Abercrombie Fox.

"Aye. She's had a rough cruise. Had a bad time of it. We've had trouble with her hands—there, what did I say?"

A confused struggle broke out forward. Figures writhed in the dim illumination and Fox heard blows and yells, and then a bellow. He saw a marine stagger back, clutching his guts.

Captain Taplow was bellowing on the instant.

Fox couldn't believe it. He refused to believe it. *Gorgon.* Well, she must have made changes, two commissions, anything could have happened. Why—they could all be dead!

He said something to Taplow, anything, it didn't matter and started forward. The confusion had sorted itself out and when Fox came up with the hatchway they were slamming the hatch covers down. Below in the gloom the glimmer of white faces stared up. Fox's face, shadowed by his new hat, must be invisible to the men penned below.

He looked down and he breathed in and stretched his lungs, and prepared to bellow in the old Foxy way.

"You see," said Captain Taplow, at his elbow. "It is quite useless to expect scum like this to be of any use."

Fox checked his bellow.

"I think, sir," he said with a grave and deliberate heaviness. "I think, sir, I might have some hope of these fellows."

"A fireship, Commander Fox? There's a guinea says you'll not move more than one of them, if that. Ha! It's a guinea you'd lose, sir, never you fear."

"It's a guinea, sir, I'll be happy to take from you."

Taplow closed his one eye. "Oh, I'll grant you that in some circumstances the scum will jump at a fireship. They think they'll get privileges. But not this lot. They've been through a bad time, sir, a bad time. They're broke."

Almost, Fox said: "If they are I'll break the bastard who broke 'em!" but he turned his fishy eye away from Taplow, and glared down into the dimness and heaved up a huge breath and he bellowed down, blasting and damning and roaring, in the good old Foxy style.

"You heaping pile of blagskites down there! You grog-faced swabs! D'you think you can skulk off and have a caulk, out of it all! Get up on deck this instant, you lay-about idle sailormen!"

Absolute silence below.

Then, a voice, a small, hesitant voice, whispering to the man's companions.

"The Cap'n . . . ?"

Another voice: "Ohmegawd! It's the Cap'n!"

Another: "It is the Cap'n—by thunder, it is!"

The gratings flew back and the men imprisoned below began to leap out on to the deck.

Taplow bellowed and marines ran to form a scarlet wall.

"Belay that," growled Fox as the bayonets came down. "There'll be no need o' that. These are *men!*"

Here they came, leaping and cavorting up on to the deck, blinking in the chill autumn light, crowding up and touching their hats, knuckling their forelocks, their faces blazing with grins and smiles that all the discipline in hell could not quench. Here they were: Barnabas, Ben Ferris, Wilson—he with the sharpest eyes in the fleet—Slattery, their American, Abdul, the enormous black man, Parsons, the cares of the world upon his shoulders, still chattering: "Ohmegawd!", Hart and Clay, Baker, they came roaring and pouring out to surround Fox.

He let them get the biliousness out of their systems for a full ten seconds. These were Raccoons, these were *his* men, and he, an officer who so dearly swore there would be no favorites in any ship he commanded—as they knew damn well and as there were not, bigod!—could not but be affected by this reunion. Then: "Silence, you blagskites." He glared about. "Where's Simpson?"

Young Ben Ferris, he whom Fox had snatched from a sinking ship in Palermo harbor, and whose mother he had seen die on the beach, said: "Simpson ain't with us, sir. He—he died, sir."

"Flogged, he was, sir," said Barnabas, towering over the others, massive, his red hair a blaze in the autumn sunlight. "Flogged around the fleet, he was, sir."

Fox felt the chill strike through. Now was no time to find out who had ordered that. Suppose that had happened to Ben Ferris, or to Parsons, his servant, always worried, always scurrying like a mouse with a waiter's bib and tucker, who could winkle out meals in the darkest of watches. My God! But wasn't it grand to have his old Raccoons back!

"You'll all be wanting to volunteer into *Nuthatch*," he told them. "Fireship. We're going in to set Johnny's breeches afire for him."

"Aye!" they shouted. Someone—anyone—bellowed out: "Three cheers for Mr. Fox!"

Barnabas quelled the incipient cheer with a shout.

"Belay that, you monkeys! Look at the Cap'n's shoulder! He's a Commander now! Three cheers for Cap'n Fox!"

They cheered.

Indeed this was a most reprehensible scene upon the miserable stinking deck of a receiving hulk. Men were running from all over thinking that the 1797 Nore was starting all over again. Fox felt light-headed. He was a black bastard—he didn't deserve men like this.

"Where's Joachim?" he shouted above the uproar.

"Please, sir," said Ben Ferris. "He's bin detailed with a party ashore, sir, seeing as he's a gunner's mate."

"Still only a gunner's mate."

"Aye, sir."

Captain Taplow was simmering away, nerving himself to interpose his fragile authority in his own ship. The marines were gaping.

Fox turned to Taplow.

"A guinea, I think you said, sir." He held out his hand, palm up, cupped.

With a poor grace Taplow fished out a guinea and dropped it into Fox's hand.

Fox spun the two coins in the air. They glittered, gold and silver. He flipped them at Barnabas.

"Share 'em out, Barnabas–and if any man o' you turns up drunk for duty he'll get–" And then Fox paused. About to bellow out in his intemperate way that a drunk would get a red-checked shirt at the gratings, he held that familiar threat in. No doubt more than one of these old Raccoons would get drunk. That was the natural way of the British seaman. But Fox would have to implement his threat. And he knew he wouldn't do it, couldn't do it–although he would, and damn quick, too, if it was a matter of vital discipline. So he changed that smoothly to: "Get the rough edge of my tongue."

Barnabas coughed and shuffled his bare feet, and said: "Beg pardon, sir; if any o' th' lads gits drunk, sir, they'll do it nice and peaceable, like, sir, begging your pardon, sir."

And they would, too. The others of his hands would see to it. Incredible–and yet true. Fox felt all the small pride of the petty-minded–and he consigned all those who called him small-minded to hell and gone. If the rest of the Navy held a tithe of what lay between him and these men, the press gangs could depart the grisly scene and never return.

"I'll not man a ship without Joachim," he said, stoutly. "And a fireship, too, into the bargain."

He made arrangements on the spot for Joachim, that stalwart German gunner's mate, to be sent across the moment he became available.

"And you're sure he will wish to volunteer, Commander Fox?" said Captain Taplow, faintly sneering.

"Another guinea on it, sir?"

"No, no," said Taplow, rather rapidly, his face pinching. "I think not."

Fox held down his guffaws until his men were pulling across to *Nuthatch.* He held down his bellows of delighted laughter until he was safely away in his cabin.

Nuthatch. Bigod! What a right and proper name that was, to be sure!

And Fox let all his mirth boil forth in a tear-bringing, gut-wrenching, shoulder-splitting gale of laughter.

Chapter Nine

"I must own, John, I find it damned peculiar. Most deuced ticklish."

"Put it out of your mind, Lionel, I beg you. I would not dream of having anything any other way."

Fox stood quietly in the darkness, eavesdropping on his officers. He had not intended to; but his habitual quiet movements had brought him on to the quarterdeck in time to hear what was clearly just one more discussion between his two lieutenants, Mr. Grey and Mr. Carker. Mr. Carker was by one week senior to Grey. Yet Grey had been already appointed as first lieutenant to Fox, and John Carker, firing up wonderfully when Fox had heaved up, to drag him off for a drink and a talk, had with a nobility that both puzzled Fox and caused him the acutest notions of admiration for the good Carker, insisted that, as he was coming as a volunteer, he would serve under Grey.

"I may try, Lionel," said Carker in that bulldog growl of his, "to tell you what I would do—you must correct me. I will not have the Cap'n's ship's discipline impaired on my account."

"And I'll try, too, to put it out of my mind, John." Grey moved in the night and Fox guessed he was rubbing a thumb down that handsome scar of his. "But, lay me horizontal, it's damnably odd!"

"Think back to the times you were sent haring into the rigging, when I was a Master's Mate and you a Mid. That should refresh your resolve."

Fox did not wish to overhear anymore. Again and again, often and often, he wondered why he, a tarpaulin old shellback, should have been blessed with two such fine officers as these. In not much else had he been blessed—in the nucleus of a crew in his old Raccoons, in his family, in his luck when it held, in this flicker of Interest he sensed building up—and he'd forgo a very great deal to keep Grey and Carker.

He went below, prepared to come up on deck again with more noise. *Nuthatch* had bucketed into a Channel Chop and by the next day they'd be up with Lymm's squadron. *Alarm* and *Firedrake* were in company, and Fox sailed at the head of two first-class officers, with a first-class crew—at last he had achieved that for which he had fought and dreamed and longed for.

And, on the morrow, he would burn it all.

No wonder he had laughed until the tears came.

Here he was, captain in his own ship, with Grey and Carker and his old Raccoons—and he was going to put a light to the match and set the whole shebang ablaze.

It was funny.

It was so damned funny it hurt.

Carker was still on half-pay, officially, there having been no time in all the rush to regulate the matter; but Fox would see to it with an energy he conceived of as an ineluctable force that Carker was officially recognized and put on full pay. They were a small bunch in *Nuthatch*, and for now that was how Fox wanted it. There would be much less business to be attended to, as there would have been a great deal—as there would be in Dawood's *Firedrake*—when it came to setting off into the bay leading to Point Avenglas.

Nuthatch sailed with a sluggish roll and an awkward twisting pitch, most uncomfortable. She was a real ship; that is, she had three masts rigged square. She had been a twenty-four gun sixth rate; but she had not been a frigate.

Built in 1760 as a deviant from the quickly abandoned Establishment of 1745, she measured one hundred and seven feet on the gun deck, and was thirty feet in the beam. Her guns had been nine-pounders, twenty-two of them on the gun deck, the remaining two amidships on the lower deck—more a series of platforms masquerading as a deck—with row ports fore and aft, in the old style even for that date. Fox felt a stab of wonder at the men who had worked her, in the old days, when even her sisters of the same class had had their oar ports moved up a deck, interspersed between the guns. What the Royal Dockyards at Deptford had done to her on her refit, he did not know; what had been done to her to make her into a fireship he most certainly did know. He had inspected the work with great thoroughness, in company with a retinue of his warrant officers: Mr. Earney the carpenter, Mr. Biggers the boatswain, Mr. Jobson the gunner. The work had been done recently enough to indicate that the navy still retained a little faith in the concept of the fireship.

The fireship had reached a zenith of power and prestige; and then had fallen away. Everyone knew what had happened to the Spanish Armada. One of the earliest uses had been by the Rhodians in 190 B.C. as mentioned by Livy. That poor devil Lieutenant Quilley, who continually quoted his Homer, and who had so uselessly died on the gangway of *Hector*, slashed down through the face by mad seaman Colum, would know all about Livy and the Rhodian fireships.

Fox was aware that the Dutch, a tough lot if ever a bunch of toughs sailed the high seas, had mightily discomfited the Prince of

Parma when he'd been besieging Antwerp in 1585. The English at the Armada had been carrying on the good work. But, of late—like the affair mentioned by Cloughton—good seamen had worked out ways of countering fireships.

A threatened ship could shift her anchorage, or the fireship could so easily be sunk by gunfire, or a daring band of men could board her and steer her clear of all danger.

Well, Fox did not intend to catch his trousers alight; but he was going to hit those Frogs in Point Avenglas—if he could. He went up on deck again, making a noise, and Grey and Carker remained silent.

Finn was on the wheel. He was not an old Raccoon; but Barnabas had vouched for him. Finn was, as his name so originally proclaimed, from Finland—now since the treaty of Nystad in 1721 freed from Russian occupation, although the Russians waited in the wings; everyone knew that. The Swedes had exhausted themselves with their many wars of the seventeenth and this centuries—for 1801 lay three months away—and Charles XII and his grand ambitions had finally allowed the Russians in. Well, Fox wished Finn well, and hoped he would fit in as a member of the crew. If he did not, may the Lord help him, GAF would not.

Fox took a turn past Finn, a big broad-shouldered man with that shock of almost white hair that denoted the old ancestry, and back, and he was balefully aware that everyone knew the captain trod his quarterdeck. Not that that meant much, for he was standing watches with Carker and Grey, they had no master's mates or midshipmen, and Ben Ferris was there filling in. Fox had great hopes for Ben if he wasn't killed.

Over the side, just visible in the star-glitter off the sea, Dawood's *Firedrake* foamed along. She was a brig, old, of course, but in essence the modern idea of what a fireship should be. Fox's *Nuthatch* represented an idea fifty years old. Fox saw the way the spume burst inboard. He had checked the light scantling decking set up between quarterdeck and forecastle to keep the water and damp away from the combustibles and the powder; but too much of this and *Nuthatch* might not burn at all.

She was not the most weatherly of ships. Yet if he shortened sail and so eased her, he'd be late getting up to the rendezvous. Well, he was the captain. He'd get there in time, and he'd get there in his own way, goddamn 'em all!

"Mr. Grey," Fox said in his mildest tone. "I'd be much obliged if you'd hand the mains'l and fores'l. Tops'ls will do us. I'm thinking."

"Aye aye, sir!" sang out Grey, and at once began bellowing through his speaking trumpet. The single bos'n's call twittered and the hands came foaming up.

My God!

How marvelous it was to hear Grey saying: "Aye aye, sir!" and to see the hands executing his commands with their lively skill, full of spirit, happy to be aboard. It gave a man things to think about, did emotions like these . . .

They'd know, those old Raccoons of his, that he wouldn't disturb them for nothing in the night watches. They'd be pleased he was easing her canvas.

So it was that after a slow passage and as the forenoon watch wore on, *Nuthatch* sailed a sea lonely, all by herself, a mere speck, until she raised the white triangles of the squadron.

If Cloughton was going to be unpleasant, Fox would have an explanation even Black Dick couldn't fault.

Wilson bellowed down the sighting.

Wilson—the fellow with the sharpest eyes in the fleet—up there in the crosstrees! It was marvelous!

Wilson added: "Flagship's signaling, sir."

Well, it would take no genius to know what that signal would be. On the instant Grey was bellowing and the hands rushed to tail on to the lifts, hoisting out the gig, holding her steady at the side as *Nuthatch* plugged along, rolling in the moderating sea, all ready to let her go when ordered.

Carker clambered into the ratlines with a telescope, the signal book under his arm. He contrived the usual miracle of maneuvering, the pages fluttering, and called down: "Our number, sir! And–" Here Carker fairly flew about with hands and telescope and book to shout down: "*Nuthatch*–appears–no–early–bird. Sir."

Confound Cloughton!

Well, Fox would brazen it out.

This time when he went aboard *Alarm* he wore his old coat, trousers, and that old and awful hat of his. He jammed the hat on his brown hair. He wouldn't like to lose that.

Almost–almost, he'd forgotten to shift his swab from his dress uniform to his undress when he'd changed earlier. Weighed down left-sidedly, he went down to report to the admiral.

"Well, sir, well?" cried Cloughton as soon as Fox appeared. "And what do you mean by being late, hey?"

Fox kept a grave and solemn face.

He could have said that there was plenty of time left to this day for them to prepare to be blown up. Instead, quite civilly, as befitted a commander speaking to an admiral, he said: "We were shipping water, sir, a considerable amount. The powder–"

"Aye aye, I understand that, Commander."

"All our copper's been taken, sir," said Fox, with something of the righteousness of an honest man accused of lechery before the congregation. "The dockyard swabs took all our copper."

"Well of course, sir! Of course! D'you think we're going to send good copper to be sunk in Johnny's front garden?"

"I don't know what the mateys took the plates off with, sir," and here Fox permitted his thin lips to rick up a fraction. "But they've fair wounded the timbers. We're taking water—we'd better make the attack tonight, sir, or we'll be awash come tomorrow."

"Use the pumps, Commander! Get the men at it! Use a few starters and get 'em a running, eh, what?"

"Aye, sir. That seems an excellent suggestion."

Black Dick stared at him. Fox guessed this old fire-eater was mulling over a few past occasions of their meetings, and wondering. Just when, Fox wondered, if ever, would he catch on to what Fox was up to? It didn't matter. Here came Sandeman, soft-voiced as ever, talking about ship's boats and marines.

Lord Lymm, thankfully, was not present.

Dawood came down and the chart was once more got out and perused, and a glass of Cloughton's rum spilled upon it, whereat he bellowed and flapped his kerchief; only a portion of the cliffs out to sea had been irredeemably ruined. They'd be going further in than that this night.

Seeing how far he could goad and push nincompoopish senior officers had hitherto been a fair game for Fox. But he owed this sick and half-drunken Cloughton a great deal. What he would have to say had to be said most tactfully. Lymm was not present, and Sandeman was making all the noises of taking on himself the command, yet—iniquitous though it was—Lymm was the senior of the two.

Fox wanted the task tonight to be done properly. He was risking his neck, and he wanted no oaf like Lord Lymm ruining all his efforts.

"Capt'n Sandeman will lead the fireships down," said Cloughton, coughing and spluttering. "Give 'em cover. Then it's tally ho for the hulk. Once she's fairly ablaze the boats can round her and make hell for leather for the frigates. Ain't that so, Captain?"

"Yes, sir. Although Lieutenant Jordan would muchly like you, sir, to reconsider his application to—"

"It ain't on, Sandeman. You must see that. Jordan can take your boats in. But Captain Lymm has to lead. He's the senior."

Fox said, most incautiously: "Captain Lymm is to lead the boats in person, sir?"

Cloughton swung his jowly face at Fox, all scarlet and quivering. "A captain's got to do it, young Fox. And Lymm's made a botch—" He stopped then, coughing. Fox saw that the coughing was a pretence. Cloughton was about to say more than he should. He choked and spluttered and finished: "I want those two Frog frigates cut out! If we can't bring 'em out—burn 'em! Is that quite clear?"

The penalties for failure were too terrible to contemplate.

There remained a quantity of further orders, to do mainly with signals, and the state of the tide must be consulted, the moon, what the confoundedly unpredictable weather would do and finally an awkward rearrangement of boats when one was discovered to be stoved. By the time Fox felt reasonably sure that the others had a rough idea of all that was involved, he took himself off back to his own command.

Even as Josephs at stroke hauled with such a massive bunching of brawny arms, and the old familiar faces showed in the boat, Fox had the glimmerings that this night's expedition would not go as Sir Richard Cloughton, Rear-Admiral of the Blue, propounded.

Fox coxed the gig himself.

Pike had been detached about some business under orders that had caused Cloughton to bellow; but with *Pike* went Tredowan, and Tarpy and Taffy, the tuneful duo, and the others of Fox's survivors from *Minion*. The other Minions who had been stripped from him before the first and useless assault by Lymm on Point Avenglas were still in the various gun-vessels of the squadron. Fox wondered just what dark and devious schemes he would have to adopt to get them back when the time came.

Once a captain signed a man into his muster book, he was most loath to sign him out.

Mind you, those gun-vessel captains had as yet no real right to sign the Minions on. H'mm. There would be no point in asking for them now, with consequent unpleasantness, for by tomorrow *Nuthatch* would be a burned cinder. No—there had to be a more cunning way to work this one.

Dawood would be getting his superfluous men out of his brig, and like *Nuthatch*, *Firedrake* would go down in flames having had as few men as possible aboard.

The gig sucked free of the water. Men scurried about the deck of the fireship. Fox stepped on to his quarterdeck.

"Very well," he said, to no one in particular. "We've a lot to do. Come on, you Nuthouses, let's get to it."

Chapter Ten

A fireship might be hurriedly improvised, of course; but if the floating pyrotechnic was to be ensured of the utmost chance of success, then a chosen ship must be most carefully prepared.

The gunner, Mr. Jobson, who had served in *Nuthatch* for some time, appeared to take the point that Commander Fox put great store by this gunner's mate Joachim. Jobson shared similar feelings with the Boatswain, Mr. Biggers, and the carpenter, Mr. Earney–and particularly with the master, Mr. Jarvis–that once they had put their old ship into her final state they would be shipped across to *Alarm*. The warrant officers had made their formal and essential request to remain aboard as volunteers.

Fox could afford to be expansive.

"No, no, gentlemen," he said, almost letting a beam broaden that cruel mouth of his. "I assure you, I shall be capitally served. You must take to the boat the instant I give you the orders."

"Aye aye, sir," they said. They were not sorry.

The scantlings between forecastle and quarterdeck came up in a great wrenching and splintering. They were no longer wanted, for the sea had indeed moderated and there was no longer the chance that water would slop inboard and ruin the combustibles and powder. As much air as possible was required to flow through the ship. The work done in the dockyard had been done well. The lower deck oar ports had been cut and enlarged into regular ports. All their port lids and the port lids of the gunless upper deck ports were hinged downwards, instead as was normal upwards. If the flames ate the fastenings through the lids would fall down away from the ports and so not obstruct the flow of air to the flames. Or stop the flames gouting out.

The upper deck itself was torn up along the bulwarks, exposing the cross-hatchings of squared timbers below. The whole deck space had been gridded, and into each exactly carpentered square fitted the barrels. They would not shift. The combustibles were resin, tallow, tar and pitch. A giant fire chamber was thus created. The powder, lower down and interspersed, was so arranged as to do the most explosive destruction when it eventually blew up.

Bundles of brushwood, the bavins, were

also aboard; but Fox set more store by the combustibles and the powder.

"We'll lay the trains of powder at the last minute, Joachim," said Fox. He felt suffused with energy. How wonderful all this was, despite that it was all designed to one horrific end, the blazing destruction of his ship!

Mr. Jobson had taken in the match, and this had to be carefully measured as to time.

Fox was powerfully reminded of the time he and Joachim had hurled fused half-kegs of gunpowder at a shore gun and a corvette, out there in the Med, flinging them from a weirdly lashed up contrivance of a catapult Fox had made. Oh, yes, those had been the days.

Fox clambered about his vessel, superintending everything, making absolutely sure that everything would work.

If he, as an honest sailorman, had to burn his ship, why, then—he'd burn her good!

The day wore on and the work was done, and Fox saw that the work was good.

Then came the most unpleasant part.

"The boat waited to take the old warrant officers across to *Alarm*. The sun slid down the western sky and a chill was creeping into the air. The weather would remain fine and calm with the hint of a breeze from the west, although that would shift, of course, with the going of the sun.

Fox eyed his men.

They were drawn up at the side of the

quarterdeck, all of them except Wilson, aloft with his sharp eyes, and Ben Ferris at the wheel. Grey and Carker, their blue coats brave in the declining sun, stood to one side and slightly in the rear of Fox. He knew well they were both hoping he would overlook them.

But the unpleasant task must be faced.

"I'm calling for volunteers," said George Abercrombie Fox in his go-to-hell voice. "Men to come along o' me in a fireship and maybe scorch their privates. Now–"

Every man stepped forward.

Fox glared at them.

He swallowed. He was getting so soft and maudlin in his old age, it just wasn't true!

"Well, you pack o' lubbers–you can't all go!"

No one moved.

Was that a hint of purple and black dropping down over his left eye? Here–on the quarterdeck of his own ship with his own men standing doggedly before him?

He had more than half a mind to snap out at Grey: "You will not be going, Mr. Grey. Mr. Carker, kindly pick the hands we require."

But that would create the most infernal unpleasantness.

Not that G. A. Fox cared about unpleasantness.

But there were those he tolerated and

those he would not tolerate. He valued Grey and Carker too much for that.

The hands were shifting about now, and there was a deal of that silent-discipline muttering they still couldn't believe he could hear at this distance. Presently with a kind of worm-like shrug of the whole mass, Barnabas was more pushed forward than stepping forward of his own volition.

He stood in front of Fox, screwing his face up in uncertainty, the sunlight making his red hair a foretaste of what was to come.

Fox let him sweat. Then he grated out, "Well, Barnabas?"

"Begging your pardon, sir. But we–that is the hands, sir–we–that is–the boat's big enough for us all, sir. And there's like to be things needs to be done, like, sir."

"The size of the boat has nothing to do with it. But if this is the sincere wish of you all, then I think I might find work for all your idle hands. We'll need to trim the set o' the canvas as we go down."

"We're with you, sir!" shouted Ben Ferris, from the wheel, so gross a dereliction of duty Fox ought to have had him flogged on the spot.

"Very well. But if any o' you layabouts come to me wanting ointment for your burns–"

They roared at this, and some even took off their hats and threw them in the air.

Incredible!

Fox supposed, somewhat bemusedly, that no doubt Commander Dawood over on *Firedrake*, busy preparing his brig for the coming holocaust, must be having a similar reception. Fox was not so idiotic as to imagine himself the only officer able to get men to shout and cheer at the possibility of a hideous death by fire.

But, still and all, these men of his, these old Raccoons, that had been by turn old Furry-arses, and would soon be old Nuthouses—Nuthatches—well, they were something very special in George Abercrombie's book.

Very special indeed.

Wilson bellowed down. "Deck there! Boat from *Glowworm*!"

Fox glared again at his men, rapped: "Carry on!" and went across to see what a boat from the gun-vessel *Glowworn* wanted.

The sun shot long orange streaks into the water, and the boat danced as it swung so that the bowman could hook on.

Fox looked down into the boat. He looked, and he set his jaw and stalked away. This was intolerable!

Moments later men were leaping up on to the ripped-open decks of *Nuthatch*. Foremost came a midshipman, eager, stammering, his angular jointed figure exactly like a wooden puppet slung on strings.

Acting in his capacity as officer of the

watch, Mr. Carker gravely halted the midshipman. Fox stepped forward.

"Well, Mr. Eckersley. And what gives we Nuthouses the pleasure of your unexpected company?"

Young Eckersley wriggled with embarrassment; but he drew himself up in the way that Fox had previously admired, and he controlled his stammer, and got out: "Please, sir! Please, sir, we've obtained permission to volunteer, sir!"

"Have you, now."

Fox stared at the men coming aboard. He didn't believe he was seeing straight. There was Tredowan, his large and phlegmatic Cornish cox'n from *Minion*, there was Tarpy and there was Taffy—that musical duo—there was Landsdowne who might soon be another as good as Wilson, there were half a dozen of the best of his men from *Minion*. Tredowan and the others must have been put off by Commander Purvis of *Pike*. Now they were here, with a few of the other Minions who had been stripped from him. He breathed in deeply, and for a space there was silence inboard save for the eternal creak of the rigging, the rattling of blocks, the groaning sigh of the ship's old timbers, the rush of water overside.

"It seems, gentlemen," said Fox, half-turning to Grey and Carker, "I am running a menagerie." He turned back to the men shuffling on the precarious perches of *Nut-*

hatch's ripped up deck. "Very well. You may all volunteer. But once we are fairly navigated into the bay—you all leave! I can use you up to then—after that—you do your duty!"

"Aye aye, sir!" they shouted, waving their hats. These old Minions were as bad as the old Raccoons!

"Please, sir," Mr. Midshipman Eckersley blurted out, twitching in his excitement. "Please, sir, Mr. Blythe's compliments, sir, and he's been told off to take in one of the boats tonight. He very much regrets, sir, that he is thus unable to share the pleasure of serving with you in the coming action."

Fox gazed with great complacency upon young Eckersley. Bigod! The lad had learned how to deliver a message!

"I shall miss Mr. Blythe, Mr. Eckersley," he said. Then the old blabbermouth Fox wobbled that damned great tongue of his. "But I am heartily pleased to welcome you aboard, Mr. Eckersley."

"Yes, *sir*. Thank you, sir."

Fox had to turn about and hunch his head down between his shoulders and stalk off to his cabin. My God! What was the Service coming to! It was turning into a scented evening in Vauxhall!

One thing remained absolutely certain.

He'd take just one officer and four men. No more.

That would be the good Carker, Barnabas,

Josephs, Tredowan and–who? Ben Ferris? Yes. The lad was quick and agile and smart; he had a brain. He would make the fourth. The others would go mad. Joachim particularly. But Joachim's work would all be done. It did not need a highly professional gunner's mate to strike flint and steel and light a fuse.

Fox decided he would not think what Mr. Lionel Grey might have to say.

When the old warrant officers and the old men and the boys had left *Nuthatch* for the last time, they must have thought they left their ship in the hands of maniacs, leaving the poor old vessel crammed with hideous combustibles to the tender mercies of a gang of hard-faced rascals. Well, so his men were, bigod!–tough, rascally and just the men for the night's work.

Suppose they *had* gone for pirates in the Med...

Fox concentrated his mind.

The tides here although not the massive forty feet of the islands were still a respectable twenty feet, and the ebb and flood must be more carefully figured in. There were a number of ways of breaking a boom. This one in Point Avenglas appeared from reports to be the usual boom and barrel, chain and anchor affair. An open boat pulling hard at it would not shift it, would most likely stove in her own strakes. Cloughton had ordered the first division of boats to destroy the boom so that the following divisions, and the two fireships, might pass. The gun-vessels, dead *Minion*'s sisters, would support. Fox cherished a churlish notion that one day he'd like to cram a fireship with gunpowder almost to the exclusion of normal combustibles and set her off against a boom like this. The bang should send the boom into the air as well as the ship. This was just a day-dream of his, to be toyed with in the dark watches of the night.

Parsons scratched up a meal—and how marvelous it was to have Parsons to look after him again, with his "Ohmegawd" and his wizardry with flour and fat and unmentionables which he could whip into duffs and other delicacies! Fox had spoken with both Grey and Carker, sounding them out. Neither had, as far as he knew, served in a fireship previously. Fox had.

"Oh, I daresay a resolutely handled fireship will do some damage, sir," said Grey, cheerfully. "But there was that business back in February of '44—when Admiral Mathews had to go at the Spanish and French off Toulon—"

"More court-martials followed that," said Carker, "than there has ever been."

"Right. And the fireship did nothing. The Dons shot her to pieces and she went up with a bang."

"I'll grant you that, Lionel. But don't forget what the Dutch did to *Royal James*. Lord

Sandwich was a fine officer; but the Dutch fireships burned *Royal James*. And," Carker went on, getting fairly launched, "after Barfleur, in 1692, they sent three fireships against the Frogs and they burned two three-deckers—a capital victory."

"And one of the three was sunk by 'em, too, John."

This kind of abbreviated talk between officers was commonplace, and for Fox it gave a good indication of the way his lieutenants were thinking. It might be a good idea to enliven their minds a little more about what lay in store for them.

"Before Wolfe took Quebec," said Fox, staring meaningfully upon Grey and Carker, and knowing they were instantly aware of what he was going to say, "the French sent fireships against Admiral Saunders in the Basin of the Saint Lawrence. We could have lost the battle and perhaps the war, then, and all North America with it. But boats were sent out, the men grappled the fireships and towed them away to burn out in safety. I do not wish, gentlemen, that we should allow that to happen to us this night. I trust I make myself clear?"

"Aye aye, sir," came the two familiar reassuring voices.

George Abercrombie Fox looked upon his officers, and upon his men and upon his vessel, and he felt as reasonably satisfied as his evil and ever-scheming brain would ever allow him to feel satisfied in this never-ending search after an unattainable perfection.

As the sun slipped beneath the horizon the squadron moved in. The vessels under Lymm would be filling their boats with men. The gun-vessels would be clearing for action. Dawood in *Firedrake* would be doing all the things Fox in *Nuthatch* was doing. The squadron closed the coast as the last of the light went, guided in by a boat showing shielded lights, visible out to sea, invisible to the shore.

Occasionally the high glitter of the stars dimmed and vanished as invisible clouds drifted. Everyone spoke in that thin penetrating whisper, as though the French could hear even at this distance. Gently *Nuthatch* eased in to the coast, following *Alarm*, with *Firedrake* tagging on astern.

Two boats towed astern of *Nuthatch*. Once Fox had safely negotiated the shoals at the mouth, with the sail drill that would call for, he would send off every single man apart from Carker and the four he had chosen.

There had been ructions.

Grey's scar had shone vividly in his face, deathly pale; then he had nodded, briefly, and said: "Aye aye, sir."

Later, Carker spoke a few words to Grey; Grey could see the sense in it, for he was still not fully recovered; but it rankled Lionel Grey, rankled deeply. Fox had to brush all that aside. Bigod! Was he a wet-nurse, a nursemaid, then?

So the squadron closed Point Avenglas in darkness and in silence ready to open the ball.

Chapter Eleven

Commander George Abercrombie Fox stood with his legs wide-braced on the quarterdeck of his own command and peered ahead into the night. *Nuthatch* glided with as much silence as any sailing ship might achieve, moving steadily on into the darkness, with the dark water smoothly passing astern. Over there to larboard lay the fort with its ten thirty-six-pounders. Above, on the cliffs, was the knoll and the burrow where he and Etienne had spied out the lie of the land.

Etienne was already off and about further spying business. They'd returned their four double-barreled pistols to Cloughton, that same Black Dick who sailed ahead in *Alarm*, and that episode receded into the past with every fresh day.

Fox hoped that Angelique and Frederic had come well out of their ordeal. The dragoon sergeant had fallen to his death just over there, to larboard, where darkness shrouded the cliffs. Had all his and Etienne's brave talk of Joseph Fouché fooled the girl and the dragoon? Had they believed, or had they divined the truth? Were a thousand French soldiers and a hundred guns waiting to belch death upon them long before they could bring their unwieldy fireships in close action?

Either way, the truth became, on the instant, academic as from ahead by the boom a confused shouting arose. Pistols banged. Sharp spurts of fire dazzled across the heaving surface of the bay.

Carker swore. Grey burst out with: "God-damn the idiots! Old Boney will hear that infernal row!"

"It is high time we cleared this vessel of all who no longer have business in her," said Fox, most evilly. They'd tacked and wore and negotiated the shoals, following *Alarm* with her full and smart crew. *Firedrake* had fallen a little astern; but Dawood would be up with them instantly, breathing fire and slaughter.

"Cannot I make a last appeal to you, sir—" began Grey.

"No, Mr. Grey, you may not." Fox could see Grey's face, a gray blob. The flashes and noise from ahead increased. Soon the forts would be firing. "Get your men into the boat at once, if you please, Mr. Grey."

Grey said: "Aye aye, sir." His voice was as stiff as a boxwood hedge. Fox did not relish that, did not relish the idea of sending Grey away. He let his tongue blab again.

"By the suffering piles of the Pope! Mr. Grey! You ain't fit yet, surely, sir, you can see that! That cut on your phizog ain't something to be neglected. Kindly do me the favor of going down into the boat–"

The forts fired.

The belching of fire illuminated the waters of the bay in long encarnadined streaks. The reports followed, blending into a long rolling thunder. Fox heard, quite distinctly, a rending smash from aloft. The main topgallant mast had been hit and, although the sail had been furled, the mast might come down any second. A second crash splintered from forward.

"Goddammit to hell" raged Fox. "We're nowhere near the bastards yet and they've got our range down pat!"

Now *Alarm* was shooting back, her eighteen-pounders cracking out, larboard and starboard. They'd be doing no good at all in the physical sense, althought they might make a French gunner's mind concentrate more powerfully upon what he was doing.

And still the noise and riot of fighting continued by the boom. A gun-vessel must have passed close for a whole broadside of thirty-two-pounder carronades went off with an almighty bang. Fox swore. Now rockets were soaring from the forts. He peered ahead. Yes! Even as he looked so the whole sky ahead burst into fire. A wide all-encompassing flash of flames shot from directly ahead.

"That's the blockship!" bellowed Carker, and then the booming concussions broke about them. Where that broadside went Fox did not know. *Alarm* was still firing. The noise racketed on. The sea alongside *Nuthatch* abruptly tore itself into a frenzy of white water, twisting and foaming. The French had clumped a good half dozen roundshot in there together. The British ships bore on and then Grey was back on the quarterdeck, touching his hat in the erratic and luridly flickering lights.

"What the blue blazing hell are you doing back here, Mr. Grey? You were given strict orders to leave!"

"Aye, sir. But the boat's sunk. Roundshot took out her bottom. No one was hurt, sir—we were just about to get them down."

"Well, we've two boats, have we not, Mr. Grey?"

Grey made a gesture with his hand, just visible.

"Aye, sir. But you and Mr. Carker and the men have to get away—"

"I think you dropped a shot into the boat on purpose, Mr. Grey." Fox was fuming. "That's just your style."

"Indeed, sir, I assure you. Fortunate though the occurrence is, I had no hand in it."

"Fortunate, is it, Mr. Grey?"

Carker coughed and then the two forts and the hulk fired together and the night became hideous with the soughing sounds of roundshot tearing the air about their ears.

When some semblance of hearing could be reestablished, Fox heard Grey saying to Carker: "How long d'you give 'em, John, before they have time to heat their shot?"

"Any minute now, Lionel. Any minute."

By God! These were a couple of callous young officers he'd trained up!

Didn't they realize they stood on a floating fireship, stuffed with combustibles and powder? If a red hot shot struck them, and the ship burned . . .

"A remarkable sight, sir," commented Grey.

"Aye," grunted Fox.

Young Lionel Grey was right. The whole bay was luridly lit by the flashes of the great guns, rockets soared and burst, the water sparkled in the reflections. The noise blattered on. And, in all this inferno, the strangest part of all was that the ship in which he served was not firing back. There was no surging thump of the guns beneath his feet, no massive concussions as they fired, no taste on his tongue, bitter and exhilarating, as the powder smoke swirled.

Damned strange, to be going down into action and not to fire a shot!

"Boom's coming up, sir."

Alarm had safely gone through. In the water ahead the wrecks of boats showed, and men clinging to them, and in the vivid streaks of reflected flame the dark blob-heads of men swimming. The French gun boats had put up a struggle for their boom; it had been a quick and nasty business. Not quick enough, grumbled Fox to himself, as he snapped an order to Ben Ferris, on the wheel, to follow exactly online with *Alarm*. When the frigate could go, so could *Nuthatch*.

The darkened fireship glided on.

At the last minute Fox with that uncanny seventh sense of his knew something was not right. . . .

"Port your helm, Ben!"

"Aye aye—" Ben Ferris was yelling when *Nuthatch* jolted as though kicked below the water line. She hesitated, staggering like a horse seeking for a purchase. Her onward momentum checked. The main topgallant mast buckled and pitched on forward, entangled with the fore topgallant and brought that and the foretopmast down in a smothering ruin over the bowsprit and forecastle.

Fox leaped on his quarterdeck with animal fury.

Men ran forward with axes. Carker was up there with them . . . Ben Ferris yelled. "I followed hard on *Alarm*, Cap'n!"

"I know, Ben. I know." Fox had to control himself. *Nuthatch* was swinging broadside now. If a shot from the forts hit her she'd be raked. Carker would be working like a maniac up there, and Fox could trust him to clear the wreckage. But what a thing to happen! The idiots charged with clearing the boom had only half done their work. When *Alarm* went through the wash of the frigate had shoved the boom aside and then sucked it back. He could only follow directly on track, and the incoming boom end had fouled under his stem. By the way the ship handled the boom was still there. A wedge of wood jammed across a vessel's forefoot could take over half her speed off . . .

Here was Eckersley, disjointed and wet through.

"Please, sir. Mr. Carker's compliments and would you back the main tops'l so he can free the log, sir." Then Eckersley, jumping with excitement, added, "A bit of the boom's fixed right under us, sir, and there's a dead Frenchman squashed up betwixt!"

The ghoulish young rascal!

"Mr. Grey!" roared Fox. "Back the main tops'l!"

Well, here was where having a rudimentary crew aboard paid dividends. The old Raccoons and Minions were on the braces like a pack of monkeys. The yard came over. The sail went to the mast and Fox just hoped the damn thing would remain upright after the punishment it had taken. Slowly *Nuthatch* lost way. They had lurched to starboard and now Fox let rip a ferocious string of oaths as *Firedrake* sailed calmly past, heading neatly into the gap in the boom. Her canvas reflected the glow and shone like brass. Then a momentary darkness fell across the scene and when Fox could see again he saw a gun-vessel was burning. The flames licked up her masts and yards, outlining them in fire. Grey let out a startled exclamation.

"Poor devils!"

"They'll only be a few more in the water, Mr. Grey! Get this confounded tub heading in again!"

"Aye aye, sir!"

There was ample light now. *Firedrake* pulled ahead, the brig going three feet through the water to *Nuthatch*'s one.

Fox leaped up on to the larboard ratlines, stared ahead beyond *Firedrake*, toward the block ship. The French fired in that instant, a stream of vicious orange streaks, and moments later Fox saw the whitewater gouts lifting in the sea around the brig. He saw the scatter of boats in the water, and for a moment could not disentangle which were French and which British. Men were fighting in the boats. They were clumped together like water beetles. The flash as pistols went off, the sudden startling gleam of a cutlass or a bayonet, the frenzied movement of dark figures. Well, it didn't matter which were which; the British boat attack had failed.

The first division, charged with breaking the boom, had done that, after a fashion. But the weight of fire, the presence of the French gun boats, the probable disorganization in their own ranks, had prevented the next two divisions from following through. A battle royal was going on out there in the open waters of the bay.

In her lurching starboard lunge, *Nuthatch* had swerved off course. The two following divisions of boats were now past the remains of the boom. They were supposed to charge straight past the burning block ship and cut out the frigates.

Fox could hardly fault the officer who, seeing the fireship so inexplicably diverging from her set course, had determined to press on. He would have done the same. But it meant the British had been badly upset in the timing of their plan. Still *Nuthatch* would not answer. Still she swung further and further to starboard. Ben Ferris had the wheel hard over now to counteract that movement, and Abdul and Finn were on the wheel with him, straining with bunched muscles. What the hell was Carker up to? The remnants of the boom should have been cleared by now.

Against the burning shape of the gun-vessel Fox saw another British bun-brig pass. That was *Darter*. Lieutenant Forbes was trying to get up to the blockship. *Spanker* and *Selby*, Commanders Green and Cotton were firing, also, unless they had burned; Fox fancied the burning gun-vessel was Commander Dodson's *Glowworm*.

But the light scantlings of the gun-vessels could not stand up to the punishment the big forty-twos and thirty-sixes in the French blockship were handing out. They criss-crossed in the bay, handled superbly, trying to beat down the French fire; but they were at a tremendous disadvantage. This was how it must have been in Lymm's first abortive attack. This time, according to Cloughton—according to Fox himself—it was going to be different.

The only difference was that the disaster appeared to be the greater.

Those little gun-vessels were supposed to be merely the support force. The main first thrust was to have been delivered by the two fireships. *Alarm* had hauled her wind and very sensibly followed the plan and was heading back, past *Nuthatch*'s larboard bow. On the signal, on the very same instant, Fox saw the little glow begin on the deck of *Firedrake*.

In seconds, suddenly, ferociously, inhumanly, the brig was sheeted in flame.

The flames blazed up, roaring and spitting, lighting up everything in conjunction with the burning gun-vessel.

Blazing and aflame from stem to stern the fireship bore down on the blockship.

In that rush of illumination Fox could see the small boat struggling back away from the fireship. That would be Dawood, very pleased with himself, escaping after having sent the fireship down. He'd done his job; but he'd left the fireship very smartly indeed after firing her. But the whole stern of the brig was wrapped in flames. That was no place for any man with a healthy regard for his own skin.

Fox leaped down from the shrouds and with a curt yell to Grey to stay where he was and get the confounded ship moving again, Fox hared forward. Stumbling over the ripped-up decks was a chancy business. He rampaged on to the forecastle and saw the clustered knot of men, heaving at a spar over the starboard bow. They were grunting and yelling and heaving and nothing seemed to be happening.

"What the hell's going on here?" bellowed Fox.

Barnabas heaved up, sweating, his red hair brilliant in the fireglow. He was absolutely calm.

"Beg pardon, sir. We had the boom beamed off, sir, but a shot fair knocked us all apart, and the dangled boom flopped back, like, sir."

So that explained at least one of the thumps he'd felt poor old *Nuthatch* take.

"Where's Mr. Carker?"

For a horrible moment Fox thought . . . And then: "Here, sir."

Carker was being held up by Jimmy Croker and Slattery. They all looked like devils in the flickering light. Carker's hat was over one ear, blood—black as ink—flowed from his scalp. His eyes burned like coals in a parchment face.

"Mr. Carker! You are wounded, sir?"

"Just a scratch, sir. But it knocked us all of a heap and the spar buckled, and the boom's still fouling us. We'll have it off directly, sir."

"Go back to the quarterdeck, Mr. Carker." Fox checked. "I'd be vastly obliged, Mr. Carker, if you'd kindly step on to the quarterdeck. Mr. Grey is in need of assistance. The boom will come free directly, as you say."

"Aye aye, sir."

Fox bent his evil eye on Barnabas. "The boom *is* coming free, Barnabas?"

"Aye aye, sir. That she is." And Barnabas flew at the knot of men heaving on the end of the spar and in the same instant Fox felt the lurch and the sucking movement and heard—over all the hellish din about him—the scrape and tumble of wooden beams gashing down the side. Instantly the head of the ship flew around. He glanced back. Men were working like shovelers at the stoke holds of hell back there. In the lurid light they hauled on braces, got the yards around, the canvas bellied, sagged, drew again and filled. *Nuthatch* began to gather way in the right direction.

Up here on the forecastle Carker had worked wonders; all the wreckage of the main topgallant and the fore top and topgallant masts had been shifted. The men were rolling their eyes at him. Bigod! If he'd been here with just four hands they'd never have done it. He wondered, with a brief flash of evil intent, just who had fouled up the boom work. Lymm? Hardly. That noble poxy lord wouldn't risk his lilylivered hide in the forefront of the boats.

Shot whirred past above. They all heard the hiss as the red hot shot plunged into the water.

"Keep your heads down, you bunch of heroes," said Fox, going back.

The men cheered him at the sally. They knew, as well as he, the value of heroes on a night like this.

Back on the quarterdeck he had time to fling a quick: "Well done, Mr. Carker," and an equally quick: "Now we'll have 'em, Mr. Grey—if you keep your men at it."

"Aye aye, sir," they both said. They must think of him as a real ogre.

"Look, sir," said Grey. "Those confounded Johnnies! They're taking the brig off, damn 'em!"

"So they are, may their livers rot!" exclaimed Carker.

Fox looked.

True enough. A band of brave and daring Frenchmen had pulled up to the burning fireship and clawed her with steel hooks and were now pulling her aside. It would be touch and go. Fox worked out the angles without conscious volition; depending on the strength of the backs of the French oarsmen and the reluctance of the burning brig to deviate from her course, the wind still carrying her on despite that every shred of canvas had burned, would hinge how far they could deviate her. Fox felt they might do it. But he fancied that Dawood might yet be proved successful.

"She'll just clip the hulk's beakhead," he said, in a nice judicious way, "unless they pull harder—ah!"

For in the massive fireglow a second boat had joined the first, and was pulling with short powerful strokes of the oars. The two boats pulled frantically.

"They'll tow her clear now, sir," said Grey.

"Indeed they will." Fox looked at them. "And we're not even afire. I think, gentlemen, that we may be the cause of some concern in the breast of Admiral Cloughton."

They remained silent, looking at him. *Nuthatch* surged on. Fox looked back, deliberately. Back there the water appeared to writhe as the contending boats' crews clashed. The two attacking divisions of boats would not get through; that was clear. He wondered how Lieutenant Alfred Blythe was faring. The British gun-vessels could not pass the blockship.

He swung back. The fire on his face must turn that ugly old lump of fire-proof figure-head into something more devilish than ever climbed out of the pit.

"Gentlemen," said G. A. Fox, "it is quite clear we will have to do the job ourselves."

Chapter Twelve

Around them in the bay of Point Avenglas an inferno raged. Burning ships, wrecked ships, shattered boats, corpses drifting in the bloodied water. Guns boomed and boomed as though they would never stop. Fires roared up, revealing the whole dramatic and terrible scene in grisly detail. There was light enough for Carker to look down as Grey produced his handsome silver watch. Fox looked at them, the pair of them, bemused.

Grey looked at his watch, glanced up at Carker, who nodded.

What the hell were the two clowns up to?

Grey stepped up to Fox. He swished off his hat.

"It is just past midnight, sir."

"So it's just past midnight!"

"Yes, sir. Mr. Carker and I, sir, join—"

"Stand aside there!" roared Fox. A spatter of blocks clattered to the quarterdeck as a shot smacked home in the mizzen-top. "That was a random one, I think," said Fox, with satisfaction. "Bring her head around more—

you there, on the wheel, haul her around you spavined layabouts!"

Nuthatch's head swung until Fox was satisfied.

Grey and Carker were both looking at him, like a couple of schoolmasters concerned over an impish boy who had failed to construe his Horace. Fox glared. "So it is past midnight, Mr. Grey. Well? Mr. Carker, what is the point of this?"

"Ah, Commander Fox," said Grey. He halted as a roundshot tore across the deck like an Irish banshee at a wake. "Mr. Carker and I join together in wishing you the most happy remembrances, sir, the most sincere congratulations, the most—ah—beneficial good wishes, sir, upon the occasion of—"

A clanging booming gongnote erupted from somewhere over side and *Nuthatch* lurched, groaning, and recovered. A second shot chipped an eight-foot splinter and sent it spinning, a deadly sliver, out over the transom. The guns were now roaring in one continuous drum-roll.

"*What?*" bellowed Fox.

"Mr. Grey is trying to say, sir," shouted Carker, "that we both of us wish you the greatest felicitations—"

A roundshot whipped past, gouged a three-foot chunk from the mainmast, tumbled over the side. Almost immediately after that another shot wrecked the bitts in a fountain of flashing splinters. Fox glared at his two lieutenants. Had they taken leave of their senses?

"What the hell are you two gabbling about?"

They looked surprised.

Grey said: "You don't *know*, sir?" He turned his handsome face with that raffish scar to Carker, who wore a bandage under his hat, with the black blood drops dripping down his forehead. "He don't know, John! Don't that beat all!"

"I find it hard to credit, Lionel."

"If you two jackanapes don't stand to naval discipline and order, I'll–I'll–" Fox fumed as the roundshot tore in and his fireship rolled laboriously on and the seconds ticked away to the moment when he would set the torch to her.

"I must admit, sir," said Grey. "I had hoped we would be beautifully alight by midnight. But nothing is perfect in this sinful world."

"Aye," said Carker, with the wise look of a constipated owl. "There's nothing perfect, that's for sure."

Fox did not stamp his foot. These two maundering idiots were treating him like–like–well, hardly like the commander of a fireship which the enemy were trying to shoot into pieces and sink!

"Tell me," he said, and his tone brought them up all standing.

Carker nodded to Grey. Grey still held his

hat in his hand. Now he waved it most elegantly.

"It's your birthday, sir. Many happy returns."

Fox gaped.

His birthday!

The twenty-ninth of September, in the Year of Our Lord One thousand eight hundred.

It was, too, bigod!

"I–" said George Abercrombie Fox. "Goddammit, don't you two loons know where we are? We're in the middle of a battle! We're like to have our heads blown off, or our tripes dropped out, anything, in the next second. And you babble on about birthdays!"

"We have taken the liberty of obtaining a present for you, sir. But in view of our–ah–little exercise tonight thought it prudent to leave the trifle with our dunnage."

"Birthday! If this keeps up as hot as it is I won't see another one."

And, he supposed, that was the answer to their conduct. They'd remembered his birthday, the pair of them, Carker and Grey–and they'd bought him a present!–and in this inferno it was no great shakes any of them would ever live to see another birthday between them.

Fox was a hard man. Everyone knew that. Damnably hard. He swung his ugly face at them–and he realized with something of a shock that he only had one eye to glare at them with. Purple and black and pink obfuscated his left eye, and–and!–black and purple began to hint and prickle his right eye, subtly, dropping down–if he went blind on his own quarterdeck now that would be the absolute end of everything.

Useless to struggle against the onset of that insidious handicap. He could do nothing. In times of stress or passion or lust, that purple ring came dropping down. Well, he would have to say something to them, about the birthday nonsense. They were decent fellows, and they were all going to be killed any second–so it didn't really matter anymore.

"Mr. Grey, Mr. Carker–I–thank you. Thank you. I find it hard–"

He could see out of both eyes perfectly well.

He could see with absolute clarity.

He could see, forward on the forecastle, a glow, a flame, a writhing ghoulish flame rising.

"Fire!" he roared. "The damned Frogs have set us afire!"

The flames shot up, crackling and raging back from the forecastle. The hands were leaping back aft, over the waist, ready at the word to crowd up on to the quarterdeck.

"Goddammit to hell!" raved George Abercrombie Fox. "I wanted to set her alight myself!"

"You can't have everything in this wicked

world, sir," observed Grey. "Even on your birthday."

"Sink me!" burst out Fox. "I was looking forward to burning my own ship!"

"Boats!" screeched Mr. Eckersley, halfway up the larboard shrouds. Fox had not allowed either Wilson or Landsdowne into the tops. "Boats! Frenchies! Dozens of 'em!"

"Here they come, men!" shouted Fox. "Are we going to let Johnny tow us clear—and we still aboard?"

"No!" they shrieked at him, mad figures in the fire glow, filthy of face, wild of eye, brandishing their weapons.

"Silence, you indisciplinary swabs! What is this, a pirate ship? We'll have this done in style!"

The gunfire diminished as the French boats closed.

Fox lifted his hand, pointing. "Don't fight 'em too hard to start with. The longer they're messing about in their boats the longer the Frogs'll hold their fire."

"Capital, capital," Carker was saying.

The Frenchmen in the two boats saw that this fireship was burning only in her foreparts and, being brave men, they saw the opportunity of doing their work more efficiently. Instead of grappling and hauling desperately at the oars to tow the fireship clear of the blockship, they would board over the quarter and steer her clear. It was an admirable plan. It was much more efficient than towing. The only trouble with the French plan was—the British crew was still aboard.

In the rapid whirl of events of this flaming holocaust of a night, the men spat on their hands and gripped their weapons and looked forward to this part of the proceedings to a good bashing fight, with a great and unholy joy.

Fox could never share that primitive emotion to the fullest extent; but he knew how his men felt, and he joined them in the release of emotion in a good knock about.

The French came in over both quarters from their two boats and instantly the quarterdeck was covered with figures struggling, with pistols popping, with naked steel gleaming wickedly in the crimson light. Fox saw the fight as a most useful diversion. Under cover of the French attack he could steer *Nuthatch* with her crew of nuthouse inmates toward the gap between the stern of the blockship and the shore. Already they were well up, and, no doubt, the crew in the blockship must be puzzled that the fireship was not making directly for them, as the first one had done.

In this fight Grey used an officer's strong curved fighting sword. Fox had been very strict on Grey over that. Carker had a sword he was fond of, and Fox was possessed of a cutlass. Mind you, after what had happened to Grey he began to think he'd better invest in a proper fighting sword...

Shattered to discover a fireship ablaze with a crew still aboard, and, moreover, a crew of a ridiculous size for such a hazardous expedition, the French fought with that *élan* and abandon so characteristic. They shouted bravely and charged. The English met them with fire and steel.

One of the French—an officer with an elegance of uniform in shocking contrast to the rapscallion ruffians in their smoke-blackened rags opposed to him—yelled orders.

"Strike down the *Capitaine de brûlot!*"

Fox knew all about the Jacobin spirit, the *sans-culottes*, the way of it during the Terror.

"*Je t'ouvrirai les tripes!*" And with this gentle announcement G. A. Fox flung himself into the fray on the burning deck of his command.

Without the necessity for direct orders his men worked their fighting cunning into the pattern of the conflict so that they stood with their backs to the taffrail, their faces forward, pushing the French on. If the French gave they'd be plunged over into the waist. Plunged over into the flames. For the combustibles were going up in fine style and the licking tongues spat and curled and danced aft along the waist. The heat made the sweat pop. It slicked on cutlass hilt and half-pike. The fire-glow reflected in the eyes of the English and turned their teeth bloody red. Against the flames the French struggled and fought like black silhouettes toppling into an inferno.

"Knock 'em off the quarterdeck!" roared Fox. "Singe their bottoms for 'em!"

The shouting, the clash of steel, the slither of naked feet beat into a pandemonium, mingled with the shrieks of wounded men and the insane crackling roar of the flames.

Between beating away a half-pike, shoving his point into the throat of its wielder, skipping aside from a cutlass blow, jumping forward and grabbing the Frenchman by the shirt, dragging him forward to be impaled, Fox shot quick calculating looks forward. As a captain he had to do this kind of thing. Tredowan, now, or Barnabas—who amazingly had not lost his cutlass—or Josephs, any of them, could just pitch in and fight, bellowing and cursing and having themselves a whale of a time. But George Abercrombie was the captain of this gang of hellions; he had to think three jumps ahead.

Slattery, their wild American, held a Frenchman by the throat and tickled his ribs with his cutlass. He shouted across at Fox.

"Say, Cap'n—begging your pardon, sir—when do we git th' word to start scrapping?"

"Now!" yelled Fox. "Raccoons! Minions! Chuck the Froggies over the side! Clear 'em all out"

Then the fight really started.

Bodies went end over end into the drink. The fires belched fury upon the contorted faces, upon the gleaming eyes and frenzied bodies, upon the glitter and thrust of blades quickly sullied with blood. In an incredibly short time after Fox halooed his pack on, the quarterdeck was clear.

The men glared about, like wolves.

Ahead and to larboard the hulk lay wreathed in smoke. She had continued to fire down the bay; as soon as her officers spotted the French had not taken the fireship they would reopen. To starboard the beginning of the inlet showed white houses reflected luridly in the fireglow. Fox could even make out soldiers running there, forming up, their muskets all atwinkle. The gap between shore and blockship was perfectly adequate for a vessel to pass; but in that erratic light and in these horrific conditions, it would demand the utmost skill. Fox glanced up at his canvas. The mainmast was burning. The sails were crisping. In moments he'd have so little control poor old *Nuthatch* would be merely a floating bonfire.

"Mr. Carker! Mr. Grey! Into the boat with the hands! All of 'em—every last one—you as well, Mr. Carker!"

"But, sir—"

Fox was stripping off his undress uniform coat. He turned his face upon John Carker.

"Into the boat with you!"

"Sir!" said Lionel Grey.

"Sink me! Is this mutiny? Get down into the boat—all of you! That is an order!"

They chivvied the hands down; but Grey and Carker hovered, and there was some trouble about the hands not wanting to leave.

"She's going to blow up directly!" bellowed Fox. "Get into the boat and push off!"

"But, sir—you—?"

"I'll see her through the gap. Then I'll jump for it. I can swim back—now, get off my quarterdeck before it all goes up!"

Fox flung his coat at Carker. He whipped his hat off and hurled it at Grey. "I'll have that hat and coat in the morning!"

"This is lunacy, sir!" Grey continued to protest.

"Someone has to steer her through the gap—if she will still answer the helm! Off! *Off!*"

The blockship could no longer train her broadside guns around sufficiently to fire at *Nuthatch*; but the French had stern chasers. These opened up with a series of almighty bangs. Fox opened his mouth, bellowing unheard. He pointed to the boat.

At last, reluctantly, protesting, feeling—well, feeling what Fox would have felt in like circumstances, no doubt—Carker and Grey went down into the boat—Grey jumping in before Carker so that the one week's seniority might be honored.

Fox leaned over the taffrail—or what was left of it.

"Pull straight back to the squadron! I'll join you—I'll look out for myself—you look out for the men!"

"Aye aye, sir!"

He ran back for the wheel. The ropes had not yet burned, although fire was creeping through beneath. The pitch in the seams was bubbling already. The foremast and mainmast wrapped in pillars of flame guided him on. The whole fore part of his vessel was one mass of flames, orange and brown, black tipped, scarlet tongued, leaping and twisting and roaring. It was damned hard to breathe. He was sweating.

But—vaguely ahead he could make out the tall masts of the two French frigates.

They were why he was here, sailing an inferno.

He had to reach them. If *Nuthatch* blew up before he could grapple at least one of 'em he'd be a bitterly disappointed man. Also, come to think of it, he'd be a dead man.

His eyes were stinging abominably; but that was the fire and the heat, he could see perfectly well. His mouth gaped open, sucking for breath, the air scorching his lungs. Sweat ran down his face. His whole body was wet. He felt as though he'd been dipped in candle wax.

The three tall masts ahead were moving.

"Goddammit!" raged G. A. Fox. "The Frog's cut his cables."

The frigates had been moored in line and the nearest had cut. Fox saw the masts open out, jumping in weird distortions through the heat blasting from his fireship. They opened and then they closed into a line. The frigate was trying to haul away into the inlet. And then—glory be!—Fox saw the second set of masts, all in a neat line, turning. The six masts clumped.

Fox guffawed.

Poor Johnny Crapaud! He'd cut and the two frigates had drifted together! What a capital turn!

Now if only poor old *Nuthatch* would last!

Fox gave the wheel a very gentle turn, pulling the spokes with a sensitive touch. The stern of the ship began to swing out to larboard. More and more. Now the head was swinging over to starboard, lining up with those six entangled masts.

The wheel span free.

The tiller ropes had been burned through. But Fox thought the movement had been sufficient.

Alone on the quarterdeck of his burning ship George Abercrombie Fox drifted down, wrapped in flames, upon the foe.

Any minute now—any minute now . . .

His mind's eye flew back to that burrow beneath the knoll. As though looking down from that high eyrie he could see the bay spread out, covered with the burning and shattered wrecks of ships, of waterlogged boats, drifting with the slow turning surge of drowned bodies. He could see the two frigates, Sandeman's *Alarm* and Lymm's *Meteor*, turning away from the holocaust of fire sleeting from the blockship. He could see the English gun-vessels pirouetting and trying to get in with their short range carronades. He could see the fire and the smoke, the shattering shock of it all, as though emblazoned in the full light of day, and yet at the same time with all the mysterious ferocity and magnificence of a night action.

And, too, he could see the forts hammering their fury against the English. Destruction reigned supreme here, in Point Avenglas, holocausts of fire and slaughter. Senseless it all must appear to a detached observer, senseless and stupid and wasteful; but Fox understood better than any detached observer the hows and the whys that had brought these contending men here in this mortal hour.

As though looking down he could see the two French frigates, having cut their cables, drifting back sluggishly up the inlet. He could see an awful flame sheeted monster following them, drifting upon them casting its fiery breath into their rigging, their masts, their yards.

Directly for the two frigates Fox

steered—or had done before the tiller ropes burned. Now the soles of his feet were so hot he had to dance about. But he would not let go until he was absolutely certain that what that inspired vision had seen would come to pass.

Not until he had grappled the frigates would he go . . .

Flames spurted up all about him now.

He could see nothing ahead, now, for the flames and the smoke.

He felt the shock of collision.

He staggered, and put his foot down hard, and yelled.

The deck was so hot he wondered it had not burst into a conflagration about him and so brought about in truth his sour jests about catching his trousers alight.

But *Nuthatch* had struck the frigates.

A greater flame grew ahead.

A gout of flame, a licking scarlet tongue, abruptly burst through by the wheel. Fox staggered back and flung an arm across his face. Bigod! He'd left it late!

He ran back for the taffrail.

He was sure the frigates were grappled, he was confident they would burn.

At the taffrail he paused for a single instant to look back.

My God!

What a scene!

Flames, flames, flames. Heat, burning, coruscating, awful. Flames towered writhing into the night sky. Three ships were burning. Three ships, locked together, blazing into mutual colossal destruction.

Fox took a deep breath and dived.

In the instant he dived *Nuthatch* blew up.

He was aware of going head over heels up into the air.

The noise was so colossal he was aware of hearing nothing.

Raw fire smote against his closed eyelids.

Like a leaf, like a scarecrow in a whirlwind, like a crumpled rag tossed up from the horns of a maddened bull, Fox flew high into the air.

He had time for one thought.

This was in the real old Foxy style.

George Abercrombie had done it again.

Trust Fox to get himself blown up on his birthday.